WHEN THE HOWLING BEGAN

Angie was jerked suddenly awake. The weird sounds seemed to be coming from the little pocket of rock outside the open door. They dropped to an unearthly whimpering, then rose in a shrill banshee cry as if some lost soul wailed out there in the night.

Angie's blood congealed with fright and her throat choked closed so that she couldn't utter a sound. She lay tense beneath the covers, aware of moonlight in the doorway and that wild howling outside. Whether it was animal or human, she could not tell. . . .

Other SIGNET Books by Phyllis Whitney

Mystery
of the
Black Diamonds

by

Phyllis A. Whitney

A SIGNET BOOK
NEW AMERICAN LIBRARY
TIMES MIRROR

WITH MANY THANKS TO *Florence Crannell Means, Muriel Sibell Wolle, Joseph Ruth, and Don Saunders, whose interest and help during my visit to Colorado made this book possible*

Library of Congress Catalog Card Number: 53-8355

Map by John Gretzer

This is an authorized reprint of a hardcover edition published by The Westminster Press.

 SIGNET TRADEMARK REG. U.S. PAT. OFF. AND FOREIGN COUNTRIES
REGISTERED TRADEMARK—MARCA REGISTRADA
HECHO EN CHICAGO, U.S.A.

SIGNET, SIGNET CLASSICS, MENTOR, PLUME AND MERIDIAN BOOKS *are published by The New American Library, Inc., 1301 Avenue of the Americas, New York, New York 10019*

FIRST PRINTING, MAY, 1974

3 4 5 6 7 8 9 10 11

PRINTED IN THE UNITED STATES OF AMERICA

Contents

1

Old-Timer

There was a sign at the foot of the canyon and Angie Wetheral stopped to read it. The morning sun of Colorado was already hot upon her bare head. It touched the shiny red of short curls and brightened a sprinkling of freckles across her nose.

Her brother Mark stood with his back to her, paying no attention to the sign, his gaze fixed upon the flat checkerboard spread of the plains stretching far to the eastern horizon. Mark was dark, like their father, and though he was eleven and a year younger than Angie, he was taller by a good two inches and it always distressed her that people thought him older than she.

"Listen to this," Angie said, and read aloud the wording on the sign: " 'Gregory Canyon is named for John H. Gregory, who discovered first gold at Blackhawk, 1859.' "

Mark pushed his straw cowboy hat farther back on his head. His attention was still fixed dreamily on the yellow-brown plains, with their dotting of blue and green which meant patches of water and trees.

"The covered wagons came across those plains, Angie. It's funny how flat the land is for all those miles and then goes straight up into the Rockies." He waved a hand at the thousand-foot rock spine that towered above them. The spine was a part of the Flatiron Mountains, which made a backdrop for the town of Boulder. "Gosh, Angie, we're really in the Rocky Mountains."

7

Angie shook her head. "No, we're not. Dad said this morning that these are only the foothills. We can't even see the ranges from Boulder. Come on, Mark, let's climb up the gulch. That ought to be as good a place as any for a murder."

She hitched up her blue jeans and patted the beading on the bright-colored Indian belt she had bought yesterday, their first day in Boulder. Somehow the belt, with its pattern of winged arrows and flying birds, made her feel a part of the Western scene and very far away from New York City. The farther away from New York she got, the better she liked it. The thought of mountains to climb and canyons to explore was wonderful. She only wished they could live here for good and never go back to city pavements.

The narrow, stony path led along the right side of the gulch, winding upward through brush and around huge boulders, to disappear ahead among the pines. On the other side there were thick woods, but the hill on this side was bare and rock-strewn, with a sparse growth of pine.

Mark clambered after her on the path, his feet slipping on loose stone. A tree branch swept his straw hat from his head and he had to go back a few paces to retrieve it.

"You could push somebody off the edge up here real easy," he said, peering down into the ravine between the hills. "He'd roll right into the canyon and be killed."

Angie looked doubtfully in the direction of Mark's pointing finger. "That's not such a good idea for a murder. Too ordinary. But suppose the body was found up there on a ledge in the Flatirons? I heard a man in town say that lots of people have been killed trying to climb those rocks. Then it would look like an accident and only Mr. Guthridge Gilmore would know it was really murder."

Before Mark could press his vote for a tumble into the canyon, an unexpected voice hailed them from the hillside above.

"Hey, you kids! You planning to bump somebody off around here?"

They looked up, startled. There on the hillside, looking almost like one of the gray-brown rocks about him, sat an old man. He wore a square gray beard, and from the brown wrinkles of his face a pair of surprisingly bright blue eyes regarded them. A battered felt hat covered his head, and he wore a tan shirt and gray trousers, patched at the knees.

Mark looked up at him doubtfully, but Angie, always ready to offer her friendship, scrambled up the hillside. This was luck—to find a real old-timer.

"Whoa now, young lady," the old man cautioned her. "Come up more soft-like. You don't have to scare all the critters away."

For the first time Angie saw that the ground around the old man's vicinity was alive with tiny creatures which scrambled for the peanuts he threw them, then scampered away, leaping among the rocks. Chipmunks, they were, though she had never in her life seen so many at once.

Mark followed her more slowly, and the little creatures scurried away to watch from behind rocks, no fear in their bright, beady eyes.

"You are an old-timer, aren't you?" Angie asked.

The old man grinned and there was a flash of teeth in his grizzled beard. "About as old-timer as they come. But I asked you a question first and you haven't answered it. What's all this about murder?"

Angie explained. "I'm Angie Wetheral, and this is my brother. Our dad is Jasper Wetheral." She paused as if that explained everything, and Mark nudged her to go on when the old man gave no sign of recognizing the name.

"Jasper Wetheral is a very well known author of murder mysteries," she explained a bit reproachfully. "He wrote *Mexico Mix-Up* and *Texas Terror* and *Sinister Serenade*—that was one about Florida—and he's done five other mysteries using his detective Guthridge Gilmore."

"Six," Mark said. "Every summer we go looking for book ideas, so now he's going to do one about Colorado."

"So that," said Angie, "is why we were searching for a good place for a murder."

The old man tossed out three more peanuts and there was a scurry of activity among his furry friends. "Well, now, that makes me feel a whole sight better about you folks. I like a good mystery myself, but I got kind of worried there for a minute, hearing you talk about murder. My name's Benjamin T. Ellington and I've lived through enough years and bad times to have seen some real murder in my day. These here mountains have brought on a lot of it that wasn't just between book pages."

"Were you here when gold was discovered?" Mark asked.

It was Angie's turn to nudge. There were no limits to Mark's imagination when he really got going. "Don't be silly. Mr. Ellington would have to be a hundred and I don't think he's that old."

"Thank you kindly, ma'am." The wrinkles around the old man's eyes curved into laugh lines. "But suppose you just call me Uncle Ben like everybody does. No, son, I wasn't around when the first hard-rockers came up through these hills. They were the boys who went for gold. Fact is, silver was the metal for me. The gold fever had died out some by the time I left Iowa to come out here."

He reached behind the rock on which he sat and held up a handsome cane made of some natural brown wood. The metal of the handle caught the sunlight with a white gleam.

"That's silver," Uncle Ben said. "But silver's dead. And gold is dead too. Costs too much to get 'em out now. Just look at the mine dumps on any mountainside, with the abandoned shaft houses above them and the old wooden chutes falling to pieces. These mountains are full of ghosts. Ghosts of towns and mines and men. Your dad's come to the right place for murder."

Mark shivered in the sunlight and Angie turned away to watch the lively reality of scampering chipmunks.

"I wish I could catch one," she said.

Uncle Ben shook his head. "Feed 'em some of my peanuts, if you want. But don't let 'em touch you. For one thing, they bite real mean, and for another, they carry spotted fever and that's no good for a human."

"Just the same," Mark said, paying no attention to the little creatures at his feet, "I'll bet there's still a lot of treasure back there in the mountains. I'll bet a fellow could get rich up there."

The old man stood up, leaning on the silver-headed cane. Now they could see how tall he was, and how suddenly stern-looking. "That kind of Rocky Mountain fever's worse than the sort these critters carry. Let me tell you something, boy. Treasure's no good unless you work for it, and work hard and honestly."

"I'd work for it," Mark said, dreamy-eyed.

The old man stood very still there on the hillside and it seemed to Angie that an odd, speculative look had come into his eyes. It was as if he had thought of more than he was telling. But before he could decide whether to continue there was a sound of somebody coming down the trail and Uncle Ben's face lighted.

"That's my friend Sam Springer," he said. Using the cane to help him, he started down the hillside, but in his eagerness he stepped into a pile of loose stone that slid under his feet and threw him to one knee.

A man in dark gray trousers and shirt and a gray felt hat with some sort of official badge on the front had appeared on the path below. When Uncle Ben slipped, he came hurrying up the hillside to raise the old man to his feet.

"You all right, Uncle Ben?" he asked anxiously. "How many times have I told you you ought to stay out of these hills and stop coming up here by yourself?"

With dignity the old man drew himself away from Sam's assistance. "Sam is the park ranger," he explained to Angie and Mark. "Only sometimes he gets the idea that he's Florence Nightingale or somebody. Sam, these are my friends, Mark and Angie Wetheral. They're looking around for somebody to murder, and it strikes me they'd better not get you on their trail."

"Our dad is Jasper Wetheral," Angie said hastily. "He writes murder mysteries."

Sam whistled. "You mean those Guthridge Gilmore stories? Say, what do you know! I've read three-four of those myself." He swung around to look accusingly at Uncle Ben. "Something tells me you changed the subject. Look here now, what if you had a bad fall up here sometime when nobody was around? Broke some bones, maybe? Then what would you do?"

"I'd just whoop and holler," the old man said. "And you'd be up there on Flagstaff Mountain someplace and you'd hear me and come arunning."

"If you conked your head on a rock, you wouldn't be whooping and hollering," Sam warned. "When you going to start being sensible?"

Uncle Ben took off his hat and smoothed down his thin hair. "Always said I'd die with my boots on like a good hard-rocker. Don't take on like an old woman, Sam. I know these hills years better than you do."

"But my bones are years younger than yours," Sam reminded him.

Angie suddenly remembered Mom and certain directions she had given them. "Mark, what time is it?"

Mark looked at his birthday wrist watch and made a face at her. "It's past time. We'd better hurry."

Angie scrambled down the hillside to the path and then turned to look back at the old man. "Do you suppose Dad could talk to you sometime?" she asked. "I mean, he'll need to do loads of research before he can get down to his story. That's why he's out here. And I'll bet you could help him."

Uncle Ben made a flourish with his battered hat. "I'd be glad to, ma'am. Why don't you and your brother bring him over to my diggings? I've got a heap of truck there that might interest him. You can call up my landlady, Mrs. Cadman, and set a time any day you want."

"We sure will," Angie said. She waved good-by and turned away, conscious of Mark's critical attention. Mark always wanted to go slow about things and think for a maddeningly long time before he did anything. But if she liked someone and wanted to make friends, Angie could see no reason for holding back. If a good idea popped into her head, it seemed foolish not to act on it at once.

Sam Springer joined them on the trail. "I'll go down with you two as far as the road. So long, Uncle Ben. You think about those bones of yours and get some sense."

Uncle Ben's laugh rang out behind them with all the vigor and enjoyment of a young man over a good joke.

Angie, walking along the trail, saw the ranger shake his head in despair.

"Do you think he really means it about bringing Dad to his—his diggings?" she asked.

"Sure he means it," Sam assured her. "He likes to talk about the old days. So you two are sure enough Jasper Wetheral's kids? I suppose that detective Guthridge Gilmore will be on the trail of somebody in Colorado any minute now."

Mark paused on a turn of the downhill path. "Oh, not for a while yet. He's back in New York. He won't come west till Dad finds a murder for him to solve."

Mark always talked as though Guthridge Gilmore were a real person. Angie hoped Mr. Sam Spring would understand.

"What's a hard-rocker?" she asked as they went down the path.

"Fellow who mines hard rock," Sam told her. "You get gold and silver out of hard rock, not from soft sedimentary rock like coal. Uncle Ben came out here when he was around fifteen—back in 1889. He made his pile in silver. Struck it rich right away. By the time he was seventeen he owned three or four mines."

"My goodness!" Angie said. She did a little mental arithmetic. "That means he must be close to seventy."

"Correct," said Sam.

They'd reached the sign at the foot of the canyon where the path ended and Baseline Road curved out of Boulder up Flagstaff.

"I wouldn't mind being rich at seventeen," Mark mused. "Or maybe even sooner. Is there really gold and silver still to be found back in the mountains?"

"Plenty of it." Sam smiled. "But you'd better talk to Uncle Ben before you go getting yourself rich by the time you're seventeen. He doesn't think much of the idea and he'll tell you why plenty quick. It sure went through his hands fast. Well, here's where I'll leave you kids. Where're you staying in Boulder?"

Angie pointed toward a low ranch-style house made of red Colorado stone. "Right down there on Baseline. We've rented a house from some people who are away for the summer."

"Good for you," Sam said. "Well, watch it if you go climbing back in the hills. People are always getting lost up here and we have to turn out a posse to hunt them. Gets to be a nuisance."

He waved and turned away. They walked the short distance down Baseline toward the low, red-stone house. That red rock was one of the things that made Boulder such a pretty town and Angie was glad they could live in a house that was made of it. So far she liked everything she'd seen about Colorado. Maybe this would be more fun than any other summer place where they'd stayed. If only they didn't always have to go back to a city at the end of the summer! If only, once they got attached to a place, they didn't always have to leave it! Angie could understand how Uncle Ben felt about the mountains. From the road in front of the house she could see the whole long stretch of foothills and it gave a lift to her spirit just to look at them.

"You know what it's like?" Mark said, his eyes following the direction of her own. "It's like the curtain being down at a play. It's fun to look at the curtain, but you know all the time that something's going on behind it. The foothills are the curtain and there's something waiting for us up in the mountains behind them."

Sometimes Mark could put an idea into words better than anyone else except Dad, Angie thought. But she couldn't resist teasing him a little when he got solemn.

"Things like gold and silver?" she asked.

"Maybe. Anyway, some kind of treasure."

"I hope you're right," Angie said lightly and ran ahead of him into the house. Mark built things up in his head sometimes until he got pretty far away from what was real and solid. But when you came right down to it, he was more apt to dream than to do. Angie herself liked action.

In the middle of the Indian rug in the living room there was a square of paper with some curious scrawls on it. Angie recognized the special code that Mom used to remind herself and others of things she might otherwise forget. She went over and picked up the scrap of paper.

2

The Map

Angie studied her mother's scribble for a moment and then held the square of paper out to Mark.

"I can understand some of it, but not all. See if you can figure it out."

Mom always wrote her reminder notes in a shorthand code that she herself was not always able to translate later. This one read: "Rmbr tl A tht JJ fnd grf."

Mark puzzled, reading what he could aloud. " 'Remember tell A'—that's you, Angie—'that Jasper Junior found . . .' but what in the world is a 'grf'?"

"That's what stopped me," Angie said. "The station wagon's gone from in front of the house, so Mom must be shopping in town."

They listened a moment and heard the irregular sound of typing from the room Dad had turned into a study. That meant their father was working and mustn't be interrupted.

"We were supposed to be home sooner in order to watch Jasper Junior while Mom went shopping," Angie said. "Maybe she's left him on the terrace where Dad can see him out the window."

They went through the glass doors at the rear of the living room and stepped onto the flagged terrace. The square of sloping lawn was neatly fenced by white pickets—a good place for a small boy to play. And there, his back to them, was two-year-old Jasper, his red-gold hair shining in the sun.

Mark threw a quick look at his sister. "There's your grf!"

"Oh, no!" Angie wailed. She could see for herself the faded and battered stuffed cloth giraffe which Jasper hugged lovingly to his chest.

Shortly before they'd left New York, Jasper had dug that giraffe out of a box of old toys belonging to Angie. If it had been anything else but Waldo the Giraffe, Angie might not have minded. But Waldo had been her sleep-with toy until she was eight years old. His one ear had been the ear in which she had confided secrets she told no one else. Waldo had comforted her after spankings and kept her from feeling lonesome when the light went out at night. Not a single beautiful doll had ever taken Waldo's place in her affections and every attempt of her mother's to toss him out with the trash had met with loud protests. Even now when she was too old to carry a stuffed toy to bed with her, she couldn't get over her old feeling of affection for the giraffe.

She hadn't liked it one bit when Jasper had discovered in Waldo the same charm she herself had recognized. She'd taken the giraffe away from him and hidden it—she thought safely—against their departure for Colorado. But Jasper must have unearthed it at the last minute and somehow smuggled it along.

Now Angie pounced on him indignantly. "Jasper, no! You can't have Waldo. I told you that before."

Jasper looked up at her with stormy blue eyes and pounded his heels on the tile of the terrace. Jasper had a very short temper.

"Oh, let him have the moth-eaten old thing!" Mark said.

But Angie took Waldo out of Jasper's clinging grasp and held the toy behind her back. Immediately screams of rage echoed out along the mountain ranges and fell upon the rooftops of Boulder. Obviously Jasper did not like being dispossessed of Waldo.

"You might as well stop yelling," Angie said firmly.

"Waldo belongs to Sister. You can't have him. You can't have him at all."

She poked unhappily at a bit of Waldo's leaking stuffing and tried to close the gap in his long, wobbly neck. And all the while the shrieks of indignation continued. Mark picked his brother up, but Jasper fought to be put down and reached wildly for the toy in Angie's hands. From inside the house came the sound of a typewriter carriage clanging its entire length. A moment later Mr. Wetheral appeared at the window of his study. His dark hair was tousled above a face that had picked up a bit of Colorado sunburn.

"What's going on here?" he shouted above the tumult being made by his younger son.

Jasper Junior cut off a shriek in the middle and stuck out his lower lip in a trembling pout. "Mister Gimmore!" he said. "Angie got Mister Gimmore!"

The three older Wetherals stared at the youngest one.

"Mister *Gimmore?*" Mark echoed. "Angie, do you suppose he's picked up Gilmore?"

"Don't be silly," said Angie. "That's Waldo. Jasper, honey, Mr. Gilmore is a character in Daddy's books. That giraffe is my Waldo and you can't have him."

Jasper leaned over in Mark's arms and plucked the giraffe out of Angie's hands. "Mister Gimmore," he announced. "Mister Gimmore knows everything."

The creator of the famous Guthridge Gilmore broke into a whoop of laughter. "Angie, your giraffe has been rechristened. Now do be a sensible girl and let Jasper have him. At your age you don't want that dilapidated wreck."

Angie winced at the term, but she knew when she was outnumbered. Her family had a complete insensitivity to her deep, though unreasonable, feelings in this matter.

"Now maybe I can get back to my nice quiet murder," Mr. Wetheral said. Mark set Jasper down on the terrace and he trotted contentedly off, hugging Waldo.

Angie, always quick to recover her good nature, remembered the news she had for her father.

"Dad," she called before he could get back to his typewriter. "We've found you a real old-timer. The park ranger told us he was a hard-rock miner in the old days and got real rich at it. And Uncle Ben says you can come to see him at his diggings any time. We're invited too."

"Well, good for you!" Dad said. "My Angie has never been known to let a blade of grass grow under her feet. The sooner the better. I'm anxious to talk to some of these old boys."

"Up there in Gregory Canyon might be a good place for your first murder," Mark said.

Dad grinned. "Don't go around town talking like that. Somebody might get the idea that I'm an undesirable citizen. Well, back to work. Keep an eye on Jasper until your mother gets home, will you?"

The two nodded, and Mark picked up a book he'd left on a terrace chair and curled himself up with it. But Angie stood where she was, her eyes still held by the long blue-green range of hills stretching north.

"I wish we could stay here," she mused aloud. "I wish we never had to go back to New York."

Mark was already deep in his book and didn't answer. Jasper was holding a conversation with Waldo Gimmore.

Angie sighed. When she and Mark had been small they'd lived for a while in New Hampshire. There had been mountains there too, right outside their windows. But then Dad began to have some success with his mystery books, and he began to do short stories for magazines and some book review work as well. He said you couldn't eat by murder alone and it was necessary to move to New York, where he could be near publishers and pick up magazine assignments. He always talked about the day when he'd have time to give to that serious novel that was growing at the back of his mind. Maybe that would be a best seller. Then he wouldn't have to write mysteries all the time and could do the novels he really wanted to do. They could live any place in the country they liked then. But first he had to get enough money ahead to be able to stop other things and work on the novel. Three growing children ate an awful lot and used up shoe leather like anything. So it didn't seem likely that Dad was ever going to get time to do the thing he wanted most to do.

Whenever she thought about that, Angie felt a little tearful. It wasn't only that she longed to live where there was plenty of outdoors and wonderful blue mountains to look at, but she felt unhappy too because her father couldn't get around to the thing that he wanted so much to do.

"What're you sniffling about?" Mark said, looking up from his book.

Angie found a handkerchief in her jeans pocket and blew her nose. "I was just thinking about Dad's novel and how he never gets time to do it."

"Maybe he will get time," Mark said. "Angie, what if we really struck color up in the mountains? Gold, or even silver. If we found treasure, maybe Dad could take it easy for a while and do what he'd really like to do."

Angie sighed again. "Oh, Mark! You sound about as sensible as Jasper. Two kids from New York aren't going to climb up in the Rockies and stumble on a fortune. Things like that don't happen in real life. Besides, a couple of million other people have been there ahead of us."

"It happened to Uncle Ben," Mark pointed out. "Say, Angie, did you notice the funny way he looked when we were talking about treasure in the mountains—as if he knew more than he was saying?"

Angie had noticed, but she didn't know what they could do about it if Uncle Ben didn't choose to speak his thoughts.

A hail from the front of the house stopped the discussion, and they hurried out to help Mom carry in the bags of groceries she'd brought from town.

Yesterday, when they'd all gone down to Pearl Street

to have a look at downtown Boulder, Mom had pur-
chased a Western sort of dress. It was light blue, with
metal studs on the pockets and down the front, and
when she put it on, Dad said he could practically hear
the jinglings of spurs. But in spite of his teasing, Angie
thought it looked nice with her mother's red hair,
which was only a shade darker than Angie's own. Mom
was wearing the dress now as she bustled around the
neat kitchen, emptying grocery bags, putting things
away. As Angie helped, she reported their climb up the
canyon and told about meeting Uncle Ben and how he
had said Dad could come over to his place and see his
things.

Mom was interested. As far as that went, she was always interested in everything—which made her most
satisfying to talk to. But now she was especially interested in hearing about Uncle Ben, and when Angie
mentioned his landlady's name, Mom dropped everything else and went right over to look Mrs. Cadman up
in the phone book.

Angie glanced at Mark and he winked at her. They
knew what was up. There was just one person in the
world of whom Mom was jealous. She was a girl
named Clara, who existed only as Mr. Guthridge Gilmore's capable and efficient secretary in the books of
Jasper Wetheral. More than anything else, Mom wanted to be in real life just as capable and efficient and
clever in helping her husband as Clara was in working
for her boss, Mr. Gilmore. Clara was always one jump
ahead in knowing exactly what Mr. Gilmore wanted.
As a result Mom was sometimes five jumps ahead of
what Dad wanted and quite often off up a trail he'd
never had any intention of climbing.

"Look, Nora, honey," Dad would say, "Clara's only
make-believe. No live woman could be as perfect as
Gilmore's secretary. I couldn't stand to have a female
like that around. I like *you* much better." But somehow
Mom had the idea in her funny red head that if she
could just be as clever as Clara, Dad would like her
even more.

So now, before Dad knew what was going on, she had called up Mrs. Cadman and made a date for Jasper Wetheral to come over to the diggings of Mr. Benjamin T. Ellington.

Thus it was that at three o'clock that very afternoon all the Wetherals, including Jasper Junior and Mr. Gimmore the giraffe, piled into the station wagon, with Mom still being Clara-efficient at the wheel, and drove over to the old part of Boulder where Uncle Ben lived.

Mrs. Cadman was out in front of the house watering the lawn. She was plump and cheerful and she took to Jasper Junior right away and was happy to keep him busy while the rest of the Wetherals called on Uncle Ben.

The old man seemed pleased to have company. He took them all upstairs to the two rooms he called his "diggings," as miners had called their claims in the old days. There was a big living room, with a smaller bedroom opening off it. The living room, Angie saw at once, was practically a museum. There were boxes of ores and samples of real gold and silver that Uncle Ben himself had mined. There was equipment for panning gold, though Uncle Ben didn't seem to have a very high opinion of anything that pertained to gold. And there was an impressive collection of old guns that interested Dad particularly.

As he showed them his things, Uncle Ben got to talking about the '80's and the early '90's when he'd come out as a boy. The gold fever had given way to a silver boom, and Ben Ellington had found himself the owner of mines, the owner of whole towns up there in the mountains.

"But I never had to work for it," he told them soberly. "It came easy and went easy. When the silver crash came, I didn't have much left. Afterward it was hard to be poor and settle down to everyday life. I'd had it easy too young. You young folks listen to me—that don't pay. A fellow only values what he has to work for and sweat over."

While he told them stories, Dad listened and Mom

sat in a corner, scribbling in a notebook. That was a trick she had picked up from Clara too. Since Dad wouldn't bother about notes at the time he should be making them, Mom felt somebody ought to take things down and see that the facts were straight. The only thing wrong with the idea was Mom's special shorthand. Sometimes it took the whole family days to figure out what the chicken tracks meant, when Mom couldn't.

From a rickety shelf Uncle Ben drew down two or three old books for Mr. Wetheral to see, and Dad promptly lost himself in an old account of gold-rush days, when men came swarming across the plains in wagons with "PIKE'S PEAK OR BUST" signs painted on them—and a lot of them had busted. Mom closed her notebook and went downstairs to see how Jasper was getting along. So that gave Angie and Mark a chance to talk to Uncle Ben by themselves. Mark lost no time in going right to the subject that interested him most.

"Could you tell us really," he said, "if there's treasure buried up in those mountains?"

"If you mean the easy-to-find gold and silver—that's gone. But now treasure—buried ..." Uncle Ben repeated the words slowly as if they made him stop and think. "Well now, boy, it's funny you should put it like that. Matter of fact, there is."

"I mean treasure somebody like us could get out," Mark said. "You see, sir, it's—" he cast a quick look in his father's direction to make sure that Dad was still absorbed in his reading, "it's pretty important that we—well, that we find a way to raise some money. Quite a lot of money."

Angie squirmed in embarrassment. Mark sounded so terribly young sometimes.

But Uncle Ben seemed not to mind. He regarded her brother soberly for a moment and one wrinkled hand stroked his gray beard. Then he crossed the room to an old-fashioned desk.

"Know where this came from?" he said, patting the

scarred wood of the desk top. "This was in an old court-house back there in the hills. It's out of a place that's no more than a ghost town now."

Dad heard the phrase and looked up from his reading. "I want to get into an old ghost town or two myself," he said. "Maybe you can tell me where I can find a few."

"Mountains are still full of 'em," Uncle Ben said sadly, "though they're tumbling down fast."

Dad returned to his reading and Uncle Ben thrust a hand into one of the crowded pigeonholes of the desk. "Let's see now. I think maybe there's something here might interest you two." He lowered his voice mysteriously, as if this was something he didn't want Dad to hear, and held out a folded sheet of paper to Mark. "Take this home with you, boy."

"What is it?" Mark asked.

Uncle Ben nodded at him solemnly. "That's your buried treasure, son. But it ain't alaying there for just anybody to pick up—the way silver was waiting for me. You got to work for it if you want it. Work with your brains and your hands. The only kind of treasure that does a man any good is the kind he works for. Put that paper away now, and you and your sister take a look at it later. See what you can make of it. It's a map—sort of. But what it means you'll have to figure out for yourselves."

Angie longed to get the paper into her own hands, but Mark, hypnotized by the old man's look and secretive tone, folded the paper carefully and put it away in his pocket. Angie promised herself that she'd keep a close watch on her brother, who was always losing things. If it was really a map of buried treasure—which seemed unlikely—she wanted to have a good look at it before he misplaced it.

She got her chance on the drive home from Uncle Ben's. Mom sat up in front with Dad and there was just Jasper and themselves—and Mr. Gimmore, of course—in the back seat. Mom and Dad were talking about Uncle Ben and the things he'd told them, so Angie nudged Mark urgently.

"Let's have a look at that map, or whatever it is."

Willingly enough, Mark took the sheet from his pocket and unfolded it. The paper looked like a piece from a school tablet, with blue lines ruled across it.

"It's not old and worn at the creases the way a treasure map should be," Mark said suspiciously. "But then, I suppose it could be a copy."

Red head touched dark as the two pored over the sheet of paper, and young Jasper began to squirm with discomfort over the crowding as he sat between them.

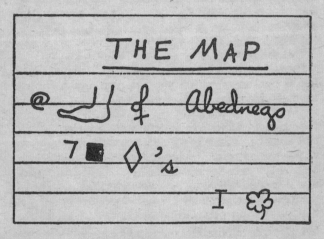

Angie took the map out of her brother's hands and settled back in her own corner of the car to study it.

It certainly wasn't a regular map. These were just symbols which Angie couldn't understand at all.

"You make any sense of it?" Mark asked. "I sure can't."

Jasper wriggled closer to Angie and bent a solemn gaze on the paper. "Mr. Gimmore knows," he announced.

Angie and Mark looked at each other and laughed.

"O.K., big boy," Mark said. "If your Mr. Gimmore knows, then how about asking him so you can tell us?"

Jasper stared at his brother for a moment. Then he picked up the limp-necked giraffe and whispered something in its only ear.

"Mr. Gimmore knows," he repeated, looking as wise as though he really had the answer.

Angie gave him a quick hug, then turned her attention back to the map. "That's an 'at' symbol and the long word is Abednego."

"Sure," Mark nodded agreement, "like in the Bible—Shadrach, Meshach, and Abednego. And that's a seven down there, and next to the flower thing is a Roman numeral one. But what does it all mean? And what has Abednego got to do with it?"

"We'll have to figure it out."

"Maybe he was just teasing us," Mark said.

But Angie would have none of that. "I think Uncle Ben is the sort of person you can trust, Mark. I'll bet anything that piece of paper means something."

"Maybe," Mark said.

Angie folded the paper carefully along the creases already made. "The thing that puzzles me most is why—if this is really a clue to treasure—wouldn't Uncle Ben go wherever it is and find it himself? Why would anybody give away a treasure map?"

"It sure seems funny," Mark agreed. "In all the books I've read everyone in the story was fighting to get hold of the treasure map. Nobody ever just turned one over to somebody else. Except maybe on a deathbed. But Uncle Ben's pretty healthy. I'll bet if he wanted to go after the treasure he could do it in a minute."

"Maybe he's found more treasure in his lifetime than he cares about. Maybe, when you're as old as he is, you don't want to be rich any more."

"Well, I care about it," Mark said, reaching for the map as Angie started to put it away in her own pocket. "Hey, give me that!"

"You lose things," Angie said calmly. "I'll put it where we can find it again."

By now the station wagon had turned up Baseline Road. Looking out the window, she could see that the Flatirons were all one gray-green color now, the way they turned in the afternoon. They were most interesting in the morning, when the sun shone on the rock precipices and made dark shadows of the gulches between.

"All out," Dad said, and Mark gave up his momentary struggle for the map.

Angie went straight into the house, with Jasper tagging along, and hid the map between her two favorite handkerchiefs. Then she went down on her knees beside Jasper and tried to explain to him again about Waldo, who was not Mr. Gimmore but the giraffe that had belonged to Sister when she was little. Jasper responded by putting Mr. Gimmore's ear in his mouth.

3

A Cry in the Canyon

In the next two weeks Angie and Mark saw quite a bit of Uncle Ben. Mom, who was always warmly interested in people, as well as eager to help Dad, had him over for dinner a couple of times. In response to her sympathetic interest, he opened up with stories about the old mining days when Central City and Leadville and Nevadaville had been bustling towns where men made fortunes—or lost their shirts. But the one thing he wouldn't open up about was the map he had given Angie and Mark.

When they teased him with questions, his bright blue eyes twinkled, but he gave them no satisfactory answers.

"If there is a treasure, why don't you go dig it out yourself?" Mark demanded more than once, but Uncle Ben's answer was always the same: "I've got all I need. I've had enough of treasure and the way it can ruin men's lives."

That seemed more reasonable than the answers he gave to other questions. When they asked why he wouldn't explain the map to them, he just shook his head and said, "It's no good unless you figure it out yourselves." When Angie asked insistently about whether he himself knew what it meant, he chuckled and repeated a phrase he had picked up from young Jasper: "Mr. Gimmore knows."

There was just one question that brought a sensible answer.

"Why did you give the map to *us?*" Mark demanded. They were out climbing Flagstaff Mountain that day and Uncle Ben turned round on the road and put one brown, wrinkled hand on Mark's shoulder. Then he reached past him to touch Angie's red hair.

"Maybe when a fellow gets to be old as me, so that all the friends he remembers are gone, maybe then the best kind of friends he can make are those as young as you are. Maybe I see something here I like. Mark's got dreams in his eyes, and Angie, you've got a heart for making friends, like your ma has. Maybe you'd do better with treasure than most folks. But only if you work for it."

Sometimes, when he talked like that, Angie almost believed that the map really did mean something. Other times she thought the old man had perhaps reached the place where he made up stories the way Mark had when he was younger; stories he really believed in himself though they bore little relation to reality. Neither Angie nor Mark, however, let Mom and Dad into the secret, knowing that their parents would regard the whole idea of buried treasure with grown-up amusement. Dad might put something like that into one of his mystery stories, but he wouldn't believe in such things in real life.

Already the Wetherals had made a couple of trips back into the mountains, in search of local color, and Uncle Ben had gone along. But what they had seen had not satisfied Dad. Central City might still boast the old Teller House and the Opera House, where New York stars came to play in the summertime. Many of the old buildings might still be standing, but it was no ghost town. It was a thriving summer city, to which tourists came from all over the country. Idaho Springs was mainly a long street of tourist camps, restaurants, and hot-dog stands, bright with neon lights and gaudy signs. Georgetown was old and picturesque, but it was decidedly alive.

"You have to get off the highways," Uncle Ben said in answer to Dad's protests. "You have to get onto the old dirt roads that nobody follows any more. I know a place. A real ghost town. Maybe I'll take you there sometime. I got to think about it awhile. Something bad happened there, and I said I'd never go back. I did once, but I don't know if I'll ever go again."

So far Uncle Ben hadn't made up his mind about taking them to the town, and Dad was waiting somewhat impatiently for his decision. Dad had some of his story figured out, but he never liked to make up the background. He wanted to present it just the way it was in real life. And he said if Uncle Ben didn't tell them where his ghost town was pretty soon, there were plenty of others they could find to have a look at. It was just that Uncle Ben kept tantalizing them all with little snatches about *his* town.

Angie could almost see the tight little valley the old man described, its steep rock wall of mountain towering on one side, with a more softly curving hillside of pines on the other. A mountain stream rushed through the valley, and Uncle Ben said you could always hear it from anywhere in town. He said you could see the snow peaks of the Continental Divide through the gap that opened out at the far end of the valley. But for some reason or other he wouldn't get down to taking them there, or even telling them the name of the town so that they could find it for themselves.

Of course Angie and Mark pondered over the map for hours at a time, and they had figured some of it out. The diamond-shaped figure had to be a diamond, of course. And the apostrophe "s" made it plural: "diamonds." It looked as if there must be seven diamonds, but what the filled-in black square meant they couldn't tell. They had also deciphered the top line as meaning, "At foot of Abednego." But who, or what, or where, Abednego was, they couldn't find out at all.

"It's probably a mountain," Mark said. And after that they searched maps and guidebooks, haunted the Boulder library, and asked every other person they met. But no one—no one at all—had ever heard of a mountain named Abednego. Angie thought it might be the name of some abandoned mine, but that trail led nowhere either. There were hundreds of peaks, hundreds of mines, back there in the mountains, so either guess might still be right.

The two symbols on which they'd given up entirely were down in the right-hand corner of the map—that Roman numeral one and the daisy, or whatever it was, that followed it. The mountains were full of flowers—but why was only *one* indicated on the map? And what kind of flower was it? Or did that matter?

Uncle Ben listened to their puzzling with that maddening twinkle in his eyes. But they knew by now that they'd get nothing out of him. Working at the map themselves was part of Uncle Ben's plan—if a plan there was.

One afternoon when the Wetherals had been in Boulder more than two weeks and the bright, hot sun of mid-July shone down on Colorado, Angie and Mark set off up Gregory Canyon to meet Uncle Ben on the trail. He'd promised to give them a lesson in Colorado rocks and ores and take them farther up in the foothills than they had gone before.

Across Gregory Canyon the spiny ridge of the nearest Flatiron looked like the back of some prehistoric monster, with white cloud trimmings floating above. Now and then a cooling breeze rushed down the canyon through the pines to touch their hot faces. They could hear it coming from 'way above, rustling and sighing along the mountainside. It sounded almost like a mountain stream when the wind blew hard enough.

On the trail ahead of Angie, Mark turned to wave at her. "I guess we're here first. Uncle Ben said he'd wait for us right up there where he was the first time we met him."

Angie reached her brother's side and looked around her doubtfully. The patches of red rock on the hill above looked familiar, but she wasn't sure. "Do you think this is the right place? You're the one who said you could find it."

"Of course it is," Mark said impatiently. "See that

big rock down there overhanging the gulch? That's my landmark. But it's funny Uncle Ben isn't waiting for us. He always gets places first."

Angie sat down on a rock and looked about her blissfully, drawing in a deep breath of the wonderful piny smell. There was nothing in New York that ever smelled like this, except maybe at Christmas time. As they waited, there was a sudden crashing in the brush across the gulch and Mark raised a warning finger to silence Angie.

"Look!" he whispered. "Right over there."

In an opening on the farther slope stood a doe and two fawns, still as garden statues, their ears pricked to attention. Holding her breath, Angie tiptoed after Mark to the big flat rock where they could best see across the canyon. There they stood as still as the wild creatures themselves, watching. Perhaps it was because they stood so still that they heard the faint cry from the rocky side of the gulch below them. In a second the doe and fawns were off through the woods, short blond tails twitching, black hoofs shining, as they leaped away through the brush. Mark and Angie stared at each other. Then they dropped to their knees and crawled to the very edge of the flat rock, where they could peer into the gulch below.

The faint cry came again, and Angie called back in response, but there was no further sound.

"It's Uncle Ben," Mark said with sudden assurance. "I'll bet he's had a fall just like Mr. Springer said he might. We've got to get down there. He needs us."

They found a place where the hill was earthy enough to give them a foothold and they went slipping and sliding down among rocks and scrubby brush and loose earth. Angie saw Uncle Ben first, where he lay on his back on a ledge, with the hot sun shining full down upon him, touching with light the silver of his beard.

"We're coming!" Mark called as they climbed over to where the old man lay.

"Uncle Ben, are you hurt bad?" Angie pleaded.

Withered eyelids fluttered, but he didn't open his

eyes. Mark felt cautiously beneath the faded shirt and nodded at Angie. "His heart is beating, though it's awfully faint. What shall we do?"

"This is where we whoop and holler for Sam Springer," Angie said. "Remember—that's what Uncle Ben said he'd do if he fell."

They raised the echoes with shouting and Indian calls and when they paused to listen, an answering shout came down from the mountainside above. Angie cupped her hands about her mouth and called in the direction of the shout.

"It's Uncle Ben. He's hurt bad. Come and help us."

Sam Springer's voice called back that he was coming down and Angie knelt beside the old man. "Give me his hat, Mark. It's over on that rock."

Mark got the battered felt and Angie held it above the old man's face so that it cut off the brilliant rays of the sun. But now Uncle Ben turned his head restlessly and opened his eyes. He moaned and then tried to smile as he recognized Angie.

"Let the sun come through," he said faintly. "I like to look at the sky. There ain't no sky anyplace as blue as Colorado's."

Angie lowered the shading hat and the old man looked right up into the blue over his head.

"Sam's coming down," Angie told him. "He'll be here any minute now and then you'll be all right." But she wasn't sure at all. His face was a queer gray color and drawn with pain, though his eyes were as bright as ever.

"You two have been real good friends to an old man. I'm not forgetting that. There's something for you to show what I mean." His eyelids fluttered and he moaned again.

Angie looked at Mark desperately. "Do you think we ought to move him? Maybe he's uncomfortable."

Mark pulled off his zipper jacket and put it in a roll under Uncle Ben's head. "It's not a good idea to move people when they're hurt. Not till somebody who knows gets here. That's Sam coming now."

They could hear Sam on the trail above, coming as fast as he could, crashing through the brush in his hurry. Mark climbed up where he could be seen and waved as the ranger came into sight. A few moments later Sam knelt beside Uncle Ben, talking to him soothingly, feeling his pulse.

"I used the phone I've got up there on a tree," he said. "There'll be an ambulance up Baseline Road in no time at all. Then we'll ease you out of here on a stretcher."

He did not reproach the old man for not heeding his warnings, and Angie liked Sam Springer all the better for that.

She watched him anxiously, hoping for some reassurance about Uncle Ben, but he appeared frighteningly grave.

"Look, you two," he said. "The boys with the stretcher won't know where to find us. So suppose you go down to the road and bring them up here when they reach the canyon."

Angie hated to leave Uncle Ben's side, but she knew Mr. Springer's suggestion was wise. Mark started back to the path right away, but Angie lingered for a moment longer. She put one hand gently on the old man's shoulder and he opened his eyes and looked at her.

"You have to get well fast," she said. "You're our very best friend in Colorado. You have to get well and take us up to your town in the mountains."

He looked into the distance as though he didn't really see her. "Black diamonds," he whispered. "Right where Abednego used to be."

But she didn't care about treasure just then. She only wanted that strange look to go out of Uncle Ben's eyes, so that he would again be the friend she knew.

Sam Springer pulled her up gently, but before she turned to follow Mark, the old man recognized her again and his mouth smiled thinly.

"Come visit me, Angie," he said.

"Of course," she told him, but her voice choked on

the words, and as she followed Mark back toward the road, she realized that her cheeks were wet with tears.

When they reached the clearing where cars could turn around, they waited in silence, straining for a first glimpse of the ambulance. They didn't want to talk now, or even look at each other. They heard the wail of the siren, long before it came into view, and Mark stood by the roadside waving as it drew near the foot of Gregory Canyon.

Two men in white coats got out. One was stocky and short and not very friendly.

"Another one," he said. "Why don't the greenhorns keep out of the hills?"

Angie burst indignantly into words. "This isn't any greenhorn. It's Uncle Ben Ellington and he knows the mountains better than anybody!"

The taller man was more friendly. "All right, redhead. Show us where he is. I know Uncle Ben. He never would be convinced that he was getting too old to go mountain-climbing."

Mark and Angie led the way back to the place where Sam Springer stood guard. He helped the two men get the old man onto the stretcher, but he didn't wait for them to carry the stretcher back up to the path. He came ahead to join Angie and Mark.

"You'd better go along home, kids," he said gently.

Mark's face twisted in a grimace and Angie knew that her brother felt like crying, just as she did. "Can't we go with you to the hospital and wait to find out how he is?"

Sam hesitated a moment, and then went on. "There isn't anything more to be done for Uncle Ben."

Angie gasped. "But—but just a few minutes ago he said we should come and visit him."

The ranger put an arm around Angie's shoulders. "You mustn't feel too bad about this. You know how he wanted to go—up here in the mountains with his boots on and the blue sky overhead. We'll miss him, sure; but we mustn't feel sorry for him. He had a good, long, full life."

Mark gulped and turned away as the stretcher-bearers reached the trail. But Angie stood looking after them, dry-eyed now, with a painful lump in her throat that couldn't be swallowed.

Suddenly, more than anything else, she wanted to be held tight in Mom's arms, just as though she were as little as Jasper. She could cry then as hard as she wanted to cry.

And she did cry later, with her head on Mom's shoulder and Mom's hand smoothing her ruffled hair.

"Why should it happen?" she wailed. "Why wasn't he careful? We saw him yesterday and he was looking forward to our trip today. I know he was! And now it—it's all ended."

Her mother's hand stroked on soothingly. "Nothing ends," she said. "Life goes on. Just look around you at the growing things and you'll feel it going on."

"But Uncle Ben's gone," Mark said gloomily. He had flung himself on the floor at Mom's feet, his head against her knee. Across the room their father stood before the big picture window that looked out on the mountains. He turned at Mark's words.

"*Is* he gone, Mark? Can't you see him right now just as if he were in this room?"

Mark looked at his father wonderingly. "That's only in my mind."

"And Angie's and Mom's and mine," Dad said. "And in our hearts. That's one kind of life that can go on for a long time."

That evening Angie went out on the lawn in front of the house and looked up at the black piles of mountain against the sky. Now and then lights twinkled as cars turned up the road to Flagstaff, and, in the deep, dark blue above, the stars seemed very bright and close. It was so hushed and quiet here that somehow she could feel near to great mysteries that were too big for little men to understand. The mystery of death was as big as that. The pain over Uncle Ben lessened a little and she was comforted.

4

More Maps

A week after Uncle Ben's funeral something surprising happened to the Wetherals. A lawyer whose name was Mr. Bingham phoned Dad and asked him to come over to Benjamin Ellington's rooms the following day and to bring Mark and Angie along. He didn't explain what he wanted and they were left wondering and curious.

The service for Uncle Ben had been a beautiful one held in a little red stone church in Boulder. The old man had apparently had a great many friends, and there were even those who heard about his death and came down from the mountains to pay their last respects. The mountain people brought armloads of wild flowers, and the bright blossoms seemed far more fitting than more formal blooms. Afterward Sam Springer had taken Uncle Ben away to be buried as he had wished, in a little mountain cemetery.

The day after Mr. Bingham called, Dad and Angie and Mark found themselves once more in Uncle Ben's living room. Mom had said it looked as if this was going to be a business meeting, so, though she was curious, she had stayed home with young Jasper.

Sam Springer was waiting for them at Uncle Ben's, and Angie was glad to see another friend. Mr. Bingham, who proved to be thin and stiff and dry, briskly took charge and came to the point the moment they were all settled. Though his manner of speaking was formal and filled with lawyer's words, Angie understood most of his surprising announcement. Among other bequests Uncle Ben had made to old friends, such as his silver-headed cane to Sam Springer, he had left some property to his new young friends Angela and Mark Wetheral—in care of their father, of course. This property consisted of a house and the grounds around it and was situated in the town of Blossom, Colorado.

Angie found it hard to hold back her excitement. She and Mark exchanged looks and she knew he was as thrilled as she. When Mr. Bingham wound up his legal terms, Angie squeezed her father's arm.

"If we *own* a house and land in Colorado, maybe we won't ever have to go back to New York City."

Sam Springer overheard her and shook his head. "Somebody'd better tell you right away. I'm not sure why old Ben did this. Maybe because it was all he had, and this was the only way he could show he appreciated your friendship. But Blossom is an old ghost town 'way back in the mountains. It's a tumble-down place off an old dirt road and I don't think you city folks would want to live there."

"Maybe we would," Angie said.

"Don't leap to any wild conclusions, young lady," Dad warned her, but there was a light in his eyes that Angie recognized. She had seen him look like that before when he got ready to do something everyone else thought was crazy.

"We can go up and look at this—Blossom—anyway, can't we?" Angie urged.

"Perhaps," her father said. "But don't get ahead of me. I was just wondering if this was the old town Uncle Ben told us about."

"Most likely it was," Sam said. "The cemetery where he's buried is up there."

Mr. Bingham cleared his throat and stood up. "If you don't mind, I must get back to my office. There will be a few formalities, Mr. Wetheral. If you will stop at my office in a day or two, we will bring the matter to a conclusion. I must say my deceased client, Mr. Ellington, was something of an eccentric. When he came to me to make this additional bequest in his will, I tried to dissuade him. The inheritance of such property is completely valueless. It is more likely to be an inconvenience than anything else."

"Not to me," Dad said. "The town of Blossom interests me mightily."

Mark's eyes were shining. "Of course, Dad! For your murder!"

"I beg your pardon?" said Mr. Bingham, losing his composure for the first time.

Dad's laugh did not altogether reassure him and, though the facts were quickly explained, Mr. Bingham took his departure looking as though he couldn't wait a moment longer to get out of such mad company. Everyone felt more relaxed and comfortable when he was gone.

Dad asked Sam Springer to tell him more about Blossom, but Sam said there wasn't much to tell.

"It was a busy little mining town in its day. First gold and then silver. But now it's a ghost, and probably in a few years there won't be much left of it but old timbers."

"How did it get its name?" Dad asked.

Sam knew the answer to that. "The early miners got some of their gold easy from quartz rock. Blossom rock, they called it. So they named the town Blossom. But the quartz has all been mined by now. There's nothing left but stuff that's too expensive to get out. Fact is, the gold was about gone by the time Ben got there as a boy. Everybody was complaining about the heavy black sand that got in the way when you tried to get gold. But Ben got an idea about that sand. He found it was rich in carbonate of lead carrying silver. He kept it to himself till he'd raised money enough to get his toe in the door. He ended up owning the town, and all the mines around it. But it sure isn't worth much now."

"How did he live during the last few years?" Dad asked.

"I guess he still had a few holdings other places that

trickled in a bit of income in his later years—and he held onto that. But he lost his fortune long ago. Didn't seem to care much though. He loved the mountains for themselves."

Most of Uncle Ben's everyday possessions had been left to Mrs. Cadman, and now she came in to ask Mark and Angie if there was anything of Uncle Ben's they'd like, just to remember him by. Mark picked out a small piece of ore that had flecks of gold in it and Angie chose a small bit of silver.

By this time Dad and Sam Springer had gone downstairs and Angie and Mark were alone with Mrs. Cadman. Angie drew a sheet of paper from the pocket of her dress and spread it out for Mrs. Cadman to see.

"Uncle Ben gave us this map," she told the landlady. "But we never could figure out what it meant. I've been wondering if he ever showed it to you or told you anything about it."

Mrs. Cadman found her glasses and peered at the ruled sheet of paper. Then she shook her head despairingly. "Oh, dear! Another one of those!"

"What do you mean—another one?" Mark asked.

Mrs. Cadman went over to Uncle Ben's desk and reached into one of the pigeonholes. From it she pulled out a stack of folded sheets.

"Here you are," she said.

Angie unfolded one sheet of paper after another. Every page was a duplicate of the one Uncle Ben had given them.

"But why did he make all these copies?" Mark asked in bewilderment.

"I don't know," Mrs. Cadman shrugged. "You have to remember that he was pretty old. I'm afraid he was a little bit childish about a few things. He made dozens of these maps, as he called them, and gave them out to anybody he liked. He gave me one years ago. And I'm sure most of his other friends have them too. They don't mean a thing, I'm afraid, except that he liked you."

"So that's it." Angie couldn't help the disappointment that crept into her voice. Mark said nothing at all, but his own disappointment was plain.

They went downstairs and joined the park ranger and their father at the car.

"I'm going downtown to pick up some things for your mother," Dad said. "You kids want to come along, or walk home?"

Mark looked at Angie in a signaling way and she answered for them both. "We'll walk."

When the station wagon was out of sight, they turned toward home beside Sam Springer. Once more Angie took out the map and held it open.

"Did Uncle Ben ever give you one of these?" she asked.

The ranger didn't have to give the paper a second glance. "Sure, he did."

"Did you ever get it figured out?" Mark asked eagerly.

"Guess I didn't try very hard," Sam Springer said. "I've got enough to do trying to keep tourists from burning up the woods, and looking for 'em when they get lost in the hills, without hunting up treasure."

"You don't believe there is any, do you?" Angie asked.

As he walked along beside them Sam took off his hat that had the ranger's badge on it, and rubbed the back of his head. "Well now, I don't know. In the years I knew Ben Ellington I never saw him do anything that didn't have some sense behind it. Except maybe this one thing. I never could figure out the map business. Fact is, I gave mine away to a fellow from the university a few weeks ago. He has a nose for stuff like this and I thought somebody might as well be puzzling it out."

"I'll bet it does mean something," Mark said, his dark eyes studying the rim of hills where afternoon clouds were coming up thick and fluffy-white.

"Maybe you're right," Sam Springer said. "Well, I've got an errand down this street, so here's where I leave you. Let me know if you dig up any treasure."

He waved at them and went off down the block. For a little while Angie and Mark walked on in silence, lost in their own thoughts.

At first after Uncle Ben's death, Angie hadn't wanted to think about the map or possible treasure. Such things faded in importance beside the choky feeling she got every time she realized he was gone. But after a while the words Uncle Ben had whispered up there in the canyon began returning to her mind and she had started wondering about the map again. So far she hadn't told Mark about what the old man had said before he died. It had hurt too much to talk about it. But now she wanted to tell him.

"You didn't hear what Uncle Ben said after he was hurt," she began. "You had started toward the trail. He got a funny look in his eyes as if he didn't know me any more and he said something about 'black diamonds.' "

Mark reached for the map in her hands. "*Black* diamonds? Then maybe that's what the filled-in black square on the map means—just the color black."

Angie nodded. "I think so too. But then he said something else. He said, 'Right where Abednego used to be.' That sounds as if Abednego—whatever it is—is gone now. And how can we ever find something that's gone?"

"Then it's not a mountain," Mark said. "But it could still be a mine. Or even a ghost town. Maybe that's it—an old ghost town with nothing left but timbers."

"Then why doesn't somebody recognize the name when we keep asking? I don't think that's it. But anyway I don't see how we can go hunting through all the Rocky Mountains for something or other that used to be called Abednego."

Mark stumbled over the curb as they came to a street crossing because he wasn't looking where he was going. He waved the map at his sister and gave a startling whoop.

"Angie! We don't have to hunt all through the

Rocky Mountains. Don't you see? This map tells us right where to look!"

"It doesn't tell *me* where to look," Angie said disgustedly. "What do you mean it tells *us*?"

"Right here." Mark put a finger on the lower right-hand corner where the petaled flower was drawn with the Roman numeral one before it. "Don't you see, Angie? That doesn't mean a lot of flowers. It means just one. One what, Angie?"

She stared at him blankly and then realization swept through her and some of Mark's excitement lighted her eyes. "Not blossoms, either, Mark. Just one—Blossom."

"Sure. Blossom, Colorado. Back there in the mountains where we're going. I'll bet that's why he left us a house there—so we'd get started hunting in the right place."

They had reached their own block and one look told them that Dad and the station wagon weren't home yet. They broke into a run and raced through the front door, slamming the screen behind them.

Mom was in the kitchen, slicing tomatoes into a big wooden salad bowl. Young Jasper crawled around the floor pushing a plastic fire truck from one green linoleum square to the next.

"Mom!" Angie cried. "Uncle Ben has left us some property. It's a house up in the mountains in a town called Blossom."

"And we're going up there," Mark announced. "Dad's going to take us all up there right away."

Mom paused with her paring knife in mid-air and stared at them. "Do you mind repeating that?" she said.

"Slow up," Angie told Mark. "We don't know for sure if Dad will want to go up there. It's an old ghost town, Mom, and Dad thought—that is, we thought—" Suddenly, her mother's expression made it hard to explain, and she let her words die out.

Nora Wetheral put down the knife and nodded her red head slowly so that the little curls at her temples bounced. "Don't tell me—let me guess. It would be a nice place for a murder."

"Well, sure," said Mark, getting down on his knees beside Jasper and reaching for the truck. "Dad wanted to find a real ghost town and here's one that will be partly ours. We can live right there and get the feeling of it. You know Dad likes to get the feeling of background for a book."

"I know," Mom said, and she didn't sound particularly happy. "No electricity. No screens. No gas stove. No washing machine. Maybe no water except what you haul."

"But it's an adventure, Mom," Mark protested. "And where could you find a better place for a murder?"

Mom sighed. "Sometimes I get tired of murders. Sometimes I wish your father could settle down somewhere and get to those novels he wants to do. Then we wouldn't have to keep traipsing all around the country. When he went on a vacation, it could be a vacation." A quaver came into her voice. "I like it here, Angie. I wish I had a darling little house like this that I could stay in and—and—"

She broke off to fumble for a handkerchief and Angie and Mark stared at her in horror. Mom was always a good sport. She never cried, or argued, or objected, no matter what happened, or what other people wanted her to do. Now even Jasper looked at her openmouthed and his lower lip started to quiver.

Mark got up and put his arms around his mother. "My goodness! We didn't know you felt like that. We don't want to go up to any old ghost town if you'd hate it."

Angie dropped down beside Jasper to keep him from crying, but she didn't soften as Mark had. "Yes, we do," she said firmly. When Mark looked at her in surprise, she went on. "It could be that there's buried treasure up there that Uncle Ben knew about and wanted us to find. If we found it, Dad could stop writing mysteries and work on his novel. And we could have a house, instead of living in an apartment in New York."

Mom dabbed at her eyes, hardly listening to her daughter. She was used to talk about fantastic subjects in the Wetheral family, and one buried treasure more or less didn't make much impression. When she heard the station wagon pull up outside, she blew her nose good and hard, and Angie could sense that she was bracing herself.

Dad had a big bunch of sweet peas poking out of the grocery bag he carried. He set the groceries down and lifted out the flowers and handed them to Mom. She didn't cry out with pleasure the way she usually did. She just took them and stood looking at them as if she didn't like what she saw. Dad was so full of his enthusiasm that he didn't notice.

"Have you heard the news, Nora, honey?" he asked. "About our son and daughter becoming property owners?"

"I've heard," Mom said.

Something in her tone penetrated even Dad's exuberance. He looked at her then, standing there with his flowers in her hands, not smiling or anything. And the smile faded from his own face.

"Well now, Nora," he said uneasily, "it's true that I had a sort of idea at the back of my mind. But if it's something that wouldn't suit you, if you'd feel at all bad about it . . ."

Mom raised her head and looked straight at him and her eyes were blue and bright like the Colorado sky.

"Jasper Wetheral," she said, "when do we start for the ghost town of Blossom, Colorado?"

Blossom, Colo.

5

Blossom, Colorado

They started on a Friday.

The trip through the mountains was cool, but dusty.
For a while, on the canyon road, whenever a car
passed them, going or coming, a great cloud of red dust
swept into the station wagon, so that there were threads
of it in every crease of the cushions and along every
ledge that would catch it. Goodness knows how their
lungs must look by now, Mom said.

But Dad was too cheerful and interested to worry
about his lungs. After a while they left the traveled
roads to follow an old, narrow road, where they'd have
had to back up if anyone wanted to pass them.

Eventually a quick mountain storm blew up to lay
the dust. Glassy sheets of water poured down the
mountainsides and the road turned into a small river
before them. Dad drove cautiously and Angie found
herself ducking when tiny hailstones pelted the car.

"Hope we don't run into many of these," Dad said.
"A real gully washer can be dangerous up in the mountains."

But in ten minutes it was over. The black thunder-
clouds rolled away from blue sky and for a little while
water glistened along every lodgepole pine and the
mountain flowers drank thirstily. The piny smell was
everywhere, and Angie breathed it in relief after all
that dust.

Jasper stood up in the front seat, safely braced behind his father's shoulder, clutching Mr. Gimmore,

whom he would under no circumstances leave behind. Every time one of the Wetherals saw a cow, or a chipmunk, or a horse, there was a shout of, "Look, Jasper!" and by now Angie was a little hoarse from the dust and the screaming.

She was getting tired too, and Mark took up more than his share of the back seat, so that she had to shove his feet over every once in a while. By late afternoon the road grew rutty and they were all anxious for the town of Blossom to show up before them. According to Dad's map and Sam Springer's directions, they should be there by now. They played the game of "around the next curve," until they wearied of it and began to think they were never going to arrive and that Blossom was only a name someone had made up.

Then the bumpy road curved out of a canyon with high sides of jagged red rock, and a narrow green valley opened before them. A mountain stream rushed out of the canyon, down the center of the valley, and they found a rickety wooden bridge across which Dad drove the car cautiously. Ahead of them stretched what had once been the main street of a flourishing town. Now weathered gray buildings, from which the paint had long ago peeled, leaned crazily on either side. Queer false fronts indicated the business section, and the Wetherals drove past them slowly. Beyond, the few houses that were left in the town straggled out, some of them with the roofs tumbled in, some of sturdier build, still erect and livable, for all that the windows were boarded up and the front steps rotted by the weather.

"This is Blossom," Angie said softly.

Mark stirred out of his doze in the back seat and came to life. "Mr. Sam Springer said our house was right opposite the bandstand," he reminded them.

"There's your bandstand," Dad said, nodding to the left of the car.

It was the smallest bandstand imaginable, and it had once been painted white. It stood above the stream, leaning a little tipsily as if it might topple over at any minute and be washed down to the plains.

But the Wetherals wasted no more than a glance on the bandstand. Their interest focused on the small, faded-yellow house that stood opposite. It was one story, with a peaked roof like a clown's cap over the front door. The glass of the windows was intact and there were padlocks on the side and front doors. Mr. Bingham had given Mom the keys, clucking despairingly at the thought of anyone so small and helpless-looking going to live in a town like Blossom.

Dad drove the station wagon into a weedy side yard that was graced by a single impressively tall blue spruce tree. Mom fell in love with the beautiful old tree at once, and Angie, stretching her legs to take out the kinks, was glad her mother had found something to like.

"Let's go inside and see whether or not the place is livable," Dad said. "Then we can decide about unpacking."

Fortunately they had plenty of camping equipment, due to the need for traveling cheaply when they toured the country. So they could manage, even if Blossom offered no real shelter.

The small yard was mostly dirt, with a few tired patches of mountain grass. There were occasional grayish posts which showed where a fence had stood, and in one place a few pickets leaned tiredly outward toward the road. Neither house nor yard looked appealing, but Angie nodded her satisfaction.

"A real ghost house in a ghost town," she said and was right on Dad's heels when the front door padlock was opened and the door pushed creakily in.

"Looks pretty good," Dad called back to Mom. "Come on in and have a look."

Mark squeezed past Angie and she and her mother walked in together, with Jasper a lively handful between them. He'd been quiet in the car for so long that now he wanted to run in six directions at once.

The house was simple in structure—just an oblong divided into four rooms. The wood floor beneath Angie's feet was gray and scaly, but there was still faded, water-stained paper on the walls, and the ceiling was all in one piece.

Mom stood in the middle of the floor, sniffing the musty smell of old walls, and Angie saw that Dad was watching her anxiously.

"It's just for two weeks," he reminded her. That was the promise he had made in the beginning when Mom had been such a good sport about coming up to Blossom. Angie had argued against a time limit because it meant they'd have to do their treasure hunting in a hurry—though she didn't explain her reason. But Mark felt that if you were going to find treasure, you could probably find it the first day, just as easily as in two months' time. Anyway, two weeks was to be the limit of their stay.

Mom straightened her shoulders. "It's much better than I expected," she said. "When we bring in our camp stools and the cots, it won't look quite so bare." She went to the rear door of the room and looked through it. "Well! Here's a potbellied stove with the stovepipe still in place. Now if it will only work, this will be better than trying to cook over a campfire."

The other front door next to the living room was in good condition too, though of course the whole place needed to be swept out and the floors scrubbed. The closed door off the kitchen, which must lead into the second back room, was painted a blue that time had faded to bluish-gray. It was Mark who discovered that this door had no knob and that it was locked besides.

Mom tried all the keys Mr. Bingham had given her, but there appeared to be none to fit that particular door. Dad put knee and shoulder to it and it cracked a little, but did not give. He turned away puzzled.

"I don't think it's locked," he said. "It gives at one point, but sticks higher up. Feels as though it might be bolted on the other side."

Angie ran through the living room to the second front room and found that it too had a door leading into the locked rear room. There was a dirty white china knob on this door, but though the knob turned, the door *was* locked. She dropped down on her knees and tried to peer through the keyhole, but the room on the other side had very little light filtering into it. Shadowy bulks stood in the way and there was no making out any detail. She went quickly back to the kitchen.

"That room seems to be filled with something or other," she reported. "It's not empty like the others."

"Well, let's not worry about it now," Dad said. "If you kids will get busy and help unpack some of the stuff in the car and—"

"Where's Jasper?" Mom said.

They all looked around, but both Jasper Junior and Mr. Gimmore had disappeared.

"Jasper!" Mom called. "Jasper, honey, where are you?"

Jasper's voice answered them, clearly and indignantly, from the other side of the locked blue door. "Mommy gone!" he protested. "Mommy gone!"

"My goodness," Angie said, "it sounds as if he were right in that locked-up room."

"Mommy's right here," her mother said. "Jasper, honey, how did you get in there? Tell Mommy how you got in!"

"Inna door," Jasper said. "Mommy come inna door."

Mark and Angie looked at each other. Then they streaked for the front door and went in opposite directions around the house. Angie discovered that the back of the house was almost flat against a sheer cliff of solid rock that rose above it. There were only a few inches to spare between the house and the rock, but by climbing up the rock wall a few feet to where a space widened out, Angie found that she could crawl behind the house. Beneath her was a little pocket of rock between the cliff and the house, and she jumped down into it. Mark was scrambling down the opposite wall in the same way. Once in the pocket, Jasper's means of entry was clear.

The locked-off room had a back entryway that yawned innocent of any door and opened right on this pocket of rock. Since there was obviously no need for a door here, Angie decided that the house must have been moved to this spot from somewhere else in the valley. Jasper stood in the opening and watched them wide-eyed, Mr. Gimmore clutched under his chin.

"Mommy gone," he repeated mournfully.

"Oh, Jasper!" Angie picked him up out of the doorway so she could climb into the room. "Mommy's not gone. Jasper's gone. Why didn't you stay with us?"

"Chairs," Jasper said. "Lotsa chairs."

Angie saw what he meant. The locked room was dim because the rock cliff cut off light. And bulking large, crowding it to the edge, stood piles of furniture. There was an assortment of chairs—rockers and straight chairs, chairs with leather seats, kitchen chairs, and a big armchair with its stuffing leaking out. There were other pieces of furniture too, which Angie couldn't identify in the dim light.

"What are you up to in there?" Dad called through the door. "Can't you let us in?"

Mark went over to the tarnished brass bolt that held the blue door shut and tugged it back. For some strange reason both doors had been bolted on the inside, and then the person who had taken this precaution must simply have departed through the doorless exit, leaving only the rock wall of the mountain to guard the interior of the house.

After a brief reunion with her youngest child, Mom looked around at the piles of furniture with delight. "This is wonderful. There's even an old sofa and a dresser and a highboy with drawers. Why, we can fix things up like a palace! Let's see now—we've got the living room and kitchen picked out. Suppose Dad and I take the other front room for our bedroom—"

"Look," Mark said, "here's another door."

It was a smaller door on the far side of the locked room. It too was secured with a stiff brass bolt. Mark opened it onto a sort of lean-to that had been built as an addition to the house and made an extra little room by itself.

"Here's my room," Mark cried. "Angie and Jasper can have this big one with all the furniture, if I can have this little one out here."

No one objected, and they all started back for the car, Mom keeping a firm hold on Jasper this time. But before the unloading began, Angie looked wistfully up the main street of Blossom. The tops of the mountains were touched with sunlight, but the wedge of valley was already falling into blue dusk and the houses of Blossom looked more gray and ghostly than ever.

"Couldn't we just take a quick walk before it gets dark?" Angie pleaded. "We haven't had a good look at the town, and pretty soon it will be too dark to see. We'd come right back and help."

Mom started to shake her head, but Dad was always sympathetic with the adventurous spirit and he signaled her with one eyebrow. She sighed and smiled.

"All right, Angie. You and Mark can take a fifteen-minute exploring trip, but not one second longer. We need you here. The darker it gets, the harder it will be to get things cleaned up."

Angie and Mark started off quickly, lest Mom change her mind. Jasper put up a howl because he wanted to go too, but Mom was a good distracter and she found something to interest him.

Once out of the yard, the explorers stood for a moment looking up and down the long main street that seemed to run the length of the valley. On ahead, there appeared a bulky brick building, larger than the others. Probably a school. Beyond it, where the road turned, following the stream, was a curious house with gables and eaves and a high cupola at the front.

"Do you suppose we could get into it?" Mark asked.

Angie looked at the gloomy old structure doubtfully. Somehow she had no particular taste for exploring a deserted house when the sun was going down.

"Let's wait till tomorrow," she said. "We don't have time enough now."

Mark agreed, so they turned back along the street they'd come down in the car, past the little steepled church that seemed to have been painted more recently than the rest of the buildings in the town, and on toward the false fronts of what had once been busy stores. In the old days, Dad had said, people had built up the fronts of their business sections to make them look two-storyish and more imposing than they really were. The word "Emporium" could still be made out in shabby lettering across one narrow building. Next to it, two small twin buildings were marked "Courthouse" and "Firehouse," and Angie had to chuckle over the dignified titles for such poor little shacks. Across the way, however, was a small sturdy building made from mountain stone, and they went over to have a better look at it. It had a thick, heavy wooden door which stood slightly ajar, and Angie pushed it open inquisitively. The smell was dank and musty and unpleasant and she drew back, rubbing her nose. But Mark slipped through the door ahead of her, and she went hesitantly after him.

There was a tiny hallway running across the front of the structure. At the back three small rooms opened on the hall and again the doors were of some heavy, solid wood, with iron locks and fastenings.

"Look," Mark said softly, and Angie saw that he was gazing up at a window at one end of the hall. There were iron bars across the window and Angie wriggled uncomfortably.

She knew what this was now. It had once been the town jail. And in these three tiny cells perhaps thieves and murderers had once been locked up.

"Do you know what I think?" Mark said in a spooky voice.

"Don't talk like that!" Angie said. "You give me the creeps. Let's get out of here."

"Somebody's watching us," Mark went on, lowering his voice still another notch.

Angie bolted for the last trace of daylight outside. "Don't be silly! You're just trying to scare me. Who'd be around to watch us?"

Mark followed her into the street. "I don't know.

But somebody is. I've felt eyes on us ever since we left the house."

Angie looked around uneasily. The mountain stream made a rushing sound that you heard all the time, just as Uncle Ben had said. And now and then wind sighed in the slope of pines across the valley. But there were no other sounds anywhere in this part of town. It was getting dark fast now and the ghostly houses of Blossom were slipping away into deep shadow.

"There's no one here to watch us," Angie said stoutly. "But our time's about up anyway. So let's go back and explore again tomorrow."

Mark fell into step beside her willingly enough and they hurried, their feet making a hollow sound on the wooden sidewalk of the business section. Then something rustled down in the direction of the stream, and Angie caught a glimpse of a black body slipping around the corner of a house whose roof had tumbled in.

She untensed her muscles and sighed with relief. "It's nothing but an old black dog, Mark. That's all that was watching us. Did you see it just then?"

"I saw it," Mark said. "And it wasn't any dog. I never saw a dog that looked like that."

Angie sniffed. "I suppose it was a dragon or a unicorn? You were always turning dogs and cats into those when you were little."

"I couldn't see it clearly enough to tell what it was," Mark said, "but I know a dog when I see one, and that wasn't a dog. Or a cat. Anyway, that's not what was watching us. An animal wouldn't have climbed up to look in a window of the jail."

"Oh, stop it!" Angie said. "You're always seeing things that aren't there. Let's run."

They ran all the way back to the house and arrived breathless, to find that Mom and Dad had swept out the four rooms and that now Dad was arranging the bulk of the furniture around the house to suit Mom. Jasper had been temporarily cornered in a sort of play-pen arrangement of chairs and was busily occupied trying to get out of it. Mom had found an oil lamp in the furniture room and Dad said he thought he could get it to work. In the meantime two storm lanterns had been brought from the car and set up where they could light the darkening house.

That night the Wetherals had a supper of sandwiches and cake, and drank the rest of the lemonade they'd brought in a big thermos bottle. Washing was sketchy, since they had to be careful of their water supply until they found out where to get water. The stream would do for washing purposes, but for drinking water they would need to locate one of the springs Sam Springer had mentioned.

Dad said the rule in a ghost town was to bed early and up early, so as to use the best of your daylight, and Angie groaned. If there was anything she liked it was to sleep late in the morning. But here in Colorado, the birds started singing about four o'clock, as she'd discovered in Boulder, and by five it was daylight. At least she was tired enough tonight to be willing to tumble into the cot Dad had set up in the now unlocked room. Some of the stuffed furniture had been set outside in the yard for the time being because mice had been using it for nests. The rest was all right and had been distributed around the house.

After she was in bed Angie found herself regarding the doorway open to the rock wall with some misgiving. The door itself had not been found, but Dad said the cliff made a good protection, except in a really bad storm, and everything would be all right for one night. In the cot across the room Jasper lay with his mouth slightly open, his plump cheeks rosy with sleep. When Mom came to kiss her good night and take the storm lantern out of the room, Angie noted that Mr. Gimmore lay on the floor where Jasper had pushed him out of bed after he'd fallen asleep.

When Mom had gone, Angie left her cot in the dark and went across to rescue the giraffe. She thought for a moment of taking it back to her own bed for company—at least that would keep it off the floor—but she could imagine what Mark would say if he caught her. Besides, Jasper would raise the roof in the morning if he found that Mr. Gimmore was missing. So she tucked him under the sheet beside her small brother and scooted back to her own bed. Mark was already asleep in his little lean-to room and Mom and Dad were settling down in the front bedroom. Angie closed her eyes and tried to think herself back in her comfortable bed in Boulder, where no open door looked out on the mountain night, where no eyes watched on a ghost town street and no strange black animals skulked out of sight among the ruins of an old house.

But it was Blossom, not Boulder, that haunted her thoughts, and when she tried to remember the Flatirons, only the picture of that grimy rock outside her room was clear in her memory. At that moment she was not at all sure that she liked the adventure of living in a ghost town. Two weeks might be altogether too long. If only they could find the treasure quickly!

She must have fallen asleep eventually, because she had a confused sense of being jerked suddenly awake when the howling began.

6

Thief in the Night

The weird sounds seemed to be coming from the little pocket of rock outside the open door. They dropped to an unearthly whimpering, then rose in a shrill banshee cry as if some lost soul wailed out there in the night.

Angie's blood congealed with fright and her throat choked closed so that she couldn't utter a sound. She lay tense beneath the covers, aware of moonlight in the doorway and that wild howling outside. Whether it was animal or human, she could not tell.

It must have been no more than seconds, but it seemed hours before she heard her mother call out: "Angie! Mark! Are you all right? Jasper, Jasper, what is it?"

Then her father's voice, still heavy with sleep: "Where's the flashlight? Nora, where did you put the flashlight?" And Mom answering him: "You left it in the rocking chair, dear."

A moment later Mark was out of his own bed and into Angie's room. She saw him standing where the moonlight came through the doorway and managed to find her strangled voice.

"Mark, don't stand in the light! Mark, get out of the doorway!"

Then Dad's flashlight beam swept in from the next room and he hurried to the open door. But the howling had stopped and only the sound of loose rock falling as something scrambled up the rock wall broke the night-time silence. Dad was too late to spot the intruder in the beam of his light.

Angie recovered the ability to move her legs and got out of bed to stand beside Mark as Dad flashed the light around the cliff wall. There was nothing there, of course, and the howler had escaped. Mom came padding in, her green silk dressing gown clutched about her, scuffs flapping across the floor. Her first concern was for young Jasper, still soundly asleep, his dreams undisturbed by the weird uproar. Then she looked at Angie and Mark.

"Children! No slippers! And this dirty, splintery old floor!"

"Gosh, Mom," Mark protested, "who'd think about slippers with a ghost screaming outside?"

"There aren't any ghosts, Mark," Mom said firmly. "And anyway ghosts don't scream. It was just an animal of some sort, wasn't it, Jasper? Maybe we'd better block off this doorway so nothing can get in."

Dad swung the flashlight over the rocks one last time and then switched it off. "That was no animal that I've ever heard. That was human or inhuman—and I'm not sure which."

"Your father's joking," Mom said quickly, shaking her head at him in her don't frighten the children manner.

But Mark wasn't frightened, just interested. While Dad moved a highboy over to the doorway and Mom supervised, he came over and perched on Angie's bed.

"I'll bet it's the somebody who was watching us this evening in the jail. You know what I think? I think someone knows we're up here after treasure and he's trying to scare us away."

The ice water had drained out of Angie's veins and she was now more annoyed than frightened. "Oh, Mark! You get the wildest ideas of anybody. In the first place nobody knows why we're up here—except for Dad's book. And in the second place anybody who knew about the treasure would go and dig it up themselves."

Mark paid no attention to her, but went off on another track. "I wonder what black diamonds are anyway? Are there any real ones?"

In the way a parent had of absently picking up a phrase you didn't think he'd heard, Dad said: "Black diamonds. Coal, probably. That's a nickname for coal."

"Coal!" Mark said disgustedly, and exchanged looks with Angie. In this land of gold and silver, coal was hardly romantic treasure.

Dad gave the furniture in front of the doorway a last shove. "That'll do it. It would take a mountain goat to get in over this stuff. And if anybody pushed it too hard, the clatter would wake us all up. Now get back to sleep, kids. In the morning we'll see if we can find out who it is around here that has a taste for practical jokes."

Mom kissed them both, tucked Jasper in, and followed Dad back to bed. Mr. Gimmore was on the floor again, looking a sickly green in the moonlight, his wobbly neck bent so that his head was tucked between his front legs. Angie rescued him for the second time, straightened out his neck, and thrust him back under the covers beside Jasper. She wished she could hide Waldo from Jasper for good, but she knew she could never get away with that.

Once more she settled down to go to sleep. But now she found herself listening intently to every creak and sigh. How had she ever thought the mountain night silent! A great wind seemed to be stirring through the pines, and then she realized that it was the rushing and splashing of the stream, sounding louder than ever in the darkness. But there were nearer sounds too—insects in the trees and somewhere crickets singing. It was an orchestra of sound and at last it droned her to sleep.

Birds were singing when she came partially awake the second time. They chirped to each other, sometimes melodic, sometimes squawking shrilly. A pale watercolor wash of daylight was painted across the room and Angie became aware of a queer thumping sound on the floor near the foot of her bed. Thump-thump, it went—thump-thump-thump. Drowsily she listened, not sure she really heard it. A soft sound, it was, yet with a little click to it. It wasn't anything hard striking the wood of the floor, but something soft and very persistent. Then it stopped and there was a scuttling noise like mice across the floor. Angie roused herself enough to look toward the door, but the barricade was still safely in place.

As she watched, her eyes sleep-filled, a black, shadowy something went climbing nimbly up the slanting back of a chair, leaped to the top of the highboy, and then vanished through the doorway.

A cat, Angie thought drowsily. A big black cat. But now it was nearly morning—the time she liked best to sleep—and she drowsed off into a dream in which Waldo Gimmore was sitting on her stomach and crying his own name over and over, again and again.

It was most irritating, and she opened her eyes to find sunlight in the room and Jasper Junior astride her, wailing at the top of his lungs.

"Mr. Gimmore gone!" he shrieked. "Mr. Gimmore gone!"

Angie tumbled her brother's fat little person down onto the bed beside her and tried to hush him.

"Mr. Gimmore's on the floor, Jasper. I picked him up twice in the night. You push him out of bed all the time."

"Mr. Gimmore gone!" screamed Jasper.

Dad's voice from the next room sounded peevish. "Angie, for Pete's sake give that moldy old giraffe to your brother and stop teasing him."

"I didn't take him and he's not a moldy old giraffe!" Angie cried, pushing Jasper firmly out of her bed. "Now you just go look for him like a good boy and let Sister sleep."

But Sister was not to be allowed to sleep. Jasper, crawling around on his hands and knees, covering himself with grime and picking up splinters, reported furiously that Mr. Gimmore was gone. There was nothing for the Wetherals to do but decide that Saturday morning had really come and they'd better get up and face it.

Mom found a means of distracting her youngest child, but no amount of searching turned up the giraffe. Jasper was right. Mr. Gimmore was very definitely gone.

"It was that cat," Angie said sleepily, pulling on her blue jeans. "I'll bet it carried the giraffe outside."

Mom, looking neat and trim in new Western Levi's and blue shirt, put her red head in the door. "What cat, Angie?"

"There was a big black cat in here around daylight. I heard him and I saw him jump out the door. He had a long, bushy black tail."

Dad came in, still in pajamas, the scrubby growth of new beard giving his chin a gray look.

"That's biologically interesting," he said. "A black cat with a big bushy tail. Just what sort of kitty was this? Are you sure it didn't have white stripes down its back?"

Angie blinked and reviewed the picture in her mind. It had looked like a cat and it had waved a plumy black tail. But it had been no more than a shadow flying through the door before her sleepy eyes, and even now she couldn't be sure it hadn't been part of her confused dreams. Except that Mr. Gimmore was gone, and it was unlikely that he'd walked out of the house by himself.

"Cats' tails fluff up when they get mad," she insisted. "Maybe this cat was mad about something."

Anyway she and Mark, who was now up and dressed, went outside and looked carefully around the yard and examined the rock pocket back of the house. But there was no giraffe to be found anywhere. When they went inside to report, they found Mom making coffee over canned heat, piling bread on paper plates, and setting out jam. Dad had cleared the furniture out of the rear doorway and stood looking out at the rocky cliff, shaking his head.

"You're the detective," Mom said. "You'd better save your reputation and get these mysteries figured out."

Dad came back into the kitchen. "You've got me mixed up with Guthridge Gilmore. He's the detective."

"Then for goodness' sakes put him on the job," Mom said.

Mark came to his father's aid. "Mr. Gilmore's still in New York. Dad can't get him out here until there's a murder."

"Well—any minute now." Mom sighed. "I'm not sure I want to spend another night in this place."

"Mr. Gimmore knows," Jasper Junior said, furnishing his own distracter for Mom. Then his lower lip began to tremble threateningly, as he remembered. "Mr. Gimmore gone!"

"Don't mention that name again," Mom warned the rest of them and spread a large slice of bread thick with raspberry jam and handed it to Jasper. The little boy took it and attacked in his usual bread-and-jam approach—nose first.

After breakfast—which had to be minus bacon and eggs or anything hot except coffee—Mark and Angie went outside to have a look at Blossom in broad daylight. There was nothing frightening or spooky about it now. Except for the school, the jail, the church, and that house with the elaborate cupola down the street, most of the buildings looked tumble-down and shabby. It was just an old deserted town, that was all. And there was nothing menacing about it.

Below the road the stream leaped over rocks, swirling and tumbling on its way, asparkle in the morning sunlight. On the hill across the valley pale-green patches marked the tender hue of aspens among the dark green of pines. It was altogether a peaceful and not at all alarming scene. Banshee wailing was something that belonged to nightmare dreams.

Then Mom's voice called from the doorway behind them. "Angie, is Jasper with you?"

"No, he's not," Angie said. "I thought he was in the house."

"Hurry and look for him outside," Mom directed, and Angie and Mark quickly circled the house without discovering a sign of Jasper.

"He can't be far away," Mark said. "Just so he doesn't go near the stream."

Down a block, in the direction of the house with the cupola, a cross street cut the main road, running in the direction of the stream. Angie and Mark hurried toward it, looking about them as they went and calling for Jasper. Mark was ahead of her at the corner and he stopped dead still, a shocked expression on his face.

"What's the matter?" Angie cried, hurrying to join him.

He held up a warning hand and pointed. There in a patch of grass beside the road sat Jasper, playing happily with a small black animal which pounced upon him again and again like a kitten. But this was no kitten. At the back of its head was a thick white line which divided along its back and ran down its plumy tail in two stripes.

It was not a kitten and it was not a dog. It was very much a live skunk.

7

Jinx

Angie and Mark stood where they were, staring helplessly. Finally Jasper looked up and saw them.

"Kitty!" he cried. "Nice kitty!"

The nice kitty backed off a few inches and then sprang upon Jasper playfully. Catching one leg of the little boy's jeans in sharp white teeth, he worried it as a dog might, and Jasper squealed with delight.

"Have you found him?" Mom called from the road.

Angie and Mark looked around and waved frantically, wordlessly. Mom gathered at once that something was frightfully wrong and she and Dad came running toward them. The sound of their coming distracted Jasper's playmate and he looked around at the group that stood watching him.

"Jasper, darling, come to Mommy quickly," Mom called. "Come to Mommy right away!"

Jasper smiled his welcome. "Mommy here," he said happily, and held out his hands to his new friend in order to show him to Mommy. The animal that all dreaded—all except Jasper—backed away again and stamped his forefeet sturdily on the ground. With a part of her mind Angie realized that that must have been the thumping sound she had heard near her bed the night before. The clicking would have been caused by the long nails on the creature's paws. This was the animal that had been in their room.

"Jasper!" Mom cried in a strangled voice and Dad put a quieting hand on her arm.

"Take it easy. Skunks misbehave only when they're frightened or angry. This one seems to be friendly enough, so don't go screeching and scaring him. We'll have to coax Jasper away. I wish we had that giraffe."

"Look," Mark whispered. "There's somebody coming."

Out of the house with the cupola had come a tall gray woman. Her dress was gray and shapeless, and her gray hair was pulled straight back from her forehead and wound in a skimpy knot on her neck. Her face was thin and weathered-looking and there was no friendliness in her gray eyes. She took in the group centered around Jasper with a single glance, and came toward it rapidly. A moment later she reached casually down to pick up the skunk by the loose skin at the back of his neck and held him dangling in the air like a cat.

"You don't have to worry," she said curtly. "Gold Strike's a pet."

"You mean he's been—er—dehydrated?" Dad asked.

Angie giggled nervously, but the newcomer did not seem to think it funny.

"His scent glands have been removed," she said, putting the skunk on her shoulder where he stuck his black little nose inquisitively into the knot of gray hair on her neck.

The Wetherals—all but Jasper—sighed with relief. Jasper stuck out his lower lip indignantly and Mark went over to pick him up. Mom smiled at the gaunt woman in gray. "We didn't know there was anyone else living in Blossom. It looks as if we're going to be neighbors. I'm Nora Wetheral and this is my husband. These two are Mark and Angela, and that big boy is Jasper."

"How-do-you-do," the woman said with a stiff formality that seemed out of place in this remote spot. "My name is Kobler. Mrs. Kobler. I belong in Blossom."

Plainly, Angie thought, she was hinting that they did not belong here.

Dad smiled at her reassuringly. "We'll be here only a week or two. Hope you won't mind."

Whether or not she minded she did not say. "Why are you here?" she asked directly.

Angie put a quick elbow into Mark's ribs lest he pop out with his usual announcement about looking for a nice place for a murder. Fortunately Dad got his words in first.

"I'm up here collecting a little local color for a book I'm writing," he explained.

Mrs. Kobler looked as if she did not believe a word of that. "I suppose you realize you're trespassing?"

"In a ghost town?" Mom began. "How could we be—"

Dad put a quieting hand on her arm and she subsided. Mrs. Kobler looked as if something smelled very bad indeed and it was not the skunk on her shoulder.

"This is hardly a ghost town," she said with dignity. "*We* live here. And all this property is owned. The town has never been abandoned."

That sounded a little funny, what with all those boarded-up buildings in the business section, the houses with tumbled-down roofs, and the general air of decay and wreckage. But Dad, fortunately, could be more diplomatic than redheaded Mom.

"Of course it is owned," he said soothingly. "I should have made our own position clear. Were you acquainted with Uncle Ben Ellington?"

"I knew *Mr.* Ellington very well," Mrs. Kobler said. "He is buried in the Blossom cemetery over yonder on the hill." She gestured with the hand that was not balancing the skunk.

Dad nodded. "It was Mr. Ellington who left us the property where we are now staying. So we're not breaking any law. We will try not to intrude on you in any way. However, I wonder if you can help us in the matter of locating water? A park ranger back in Boulder told us there were springs in the woods around here."

Mrs. Kobler slapped Gold Strike to keep him from nibbling her ear and nodded in the direction of the stream. "There's one across the bridge there, right up the hill. I suppose you're entitled to use it."

"Thank you," Dad said. "Now there's just one more thing I'd like to ask you about. Are there any wolves in the hills around here?"

She stared as if he'd taken leave of his senses. "Wolves? Not these days."

"Then perhaps you can tell me what sort of animal it was that came howling outside our house in the middle of the night."

For a moment longer Mrs. Kobler looked at him. Then she pulled the skunk from her shoulder, slapped him lightly again, and put him down on the ground, where he promptly started chewing on her shoelaces. She set her hands on her hips, elbows akimbo, and turned in the direction of the cupolaed house.

"Jinx!" she called in ringing tones. "Jinx Kobler, you come here this minute!"

The owner of the name had apparently been peering at them from behind a drawn blind in the front window. Now the blind fluttered, and a moment later the front door opened a crack to reveal a brown face topped with black hair.

Mrs. Kobler waited without repeating her summons. After a further moment of hesitation, the door opened wide and a girl came out and walked slowly down the steps. Angie watched with interest as she came down the road toward them. She was small-boned and tiny, but she looked as if she might be eleven or twelve. She wore patched jeans and a faded blue shirt that was clean and well pressed. Her black hair had an obvious tendency to curl into tendrils about her face, but had been slicked back and tightly bound into long thick braids.

"Come here," Mrs. Kobler said sternly.

Only the eyes seemed alive in the girl's solemn brown face. There was an independent snap to them as they stared at the woman who had summoned her, and Angie sensed that there was no love lost between these two.

"Were you out last night kicking up a commotion?" Mrs. Kobler demanded.

The girl flicked a disapproving look at the Wetherals and answered without hesitation. "Yes, Grandmother."

"Why?" asked Mrs. Kobler shortly.

Angie felt the girl's dark, intense gaze rest momentarily on herself, and then return to her grandmother's face. "I wanted to scare 'em out. We don't want none of their kind here in Blossom."

"*Any* of their kind," corrected her grandmother. "And just what business is it of yours?"

"Blossom's ours," the girl said, suddenly fierce. "Just ours."

"It has never been just ours," Mrs. Kobler reproved her. "Now you may apologize to Mr. Wetheral for frightening his family."

Jinx Kobler's sun-browned face flushed, and for a moment Angie thought she might refuse. Then she mumbled, "I'm sorry," without looking at any of them.

Her granddaughter's lack of manners apparently made Mrs. Kobler feel that she should set an example by being more cordial.

"I hope you'll enjoy your stay in Blossom," she said, with the air of one who displayed the attractions of an exclusive resort. "If there is any way I can help you, please call on me."

She listened to their thanks with her air of stern dignity and then turned back toward her own house. Jinx strolled after her, dragging scuffed loafers in the dusty road. Neither one gave the Wetherals a further glance. Gold Strike evidently knew which family he belonged to, for he scampered in Jinx's wake, his short front legs and longer back ones giving him an amusing, uneven gait.

"Well, I never!" Mom cried softly. "What a queer old woman, and what a strange child! Do you suppose they live up here all by themselves?"

"I wouldn't know," Dad said. "The woman is apparently educated. But she looks like a pretty unfeeling character. Nobody I'd want to trust with the raising of a young girl." He reached out to rumple Angie's red curls affectionately and Angie knew he was somehow sorry for that other girl. Suddenly she was sorry for Jinx herself.

Without stopping to think, or make any sensible plan, she said, "I'll be back in a minute, Mom," and ran down the road after the girl with the stiff black braids.

Mrs. Kobler had gone ahead into the house, but Jinx still scuffed listlessly through the dust, the skunk gamboling at her heels.

"Hello," Angie said and gave the other girl her biggest smile. Making friends was the thing she did most easily. She liked people and she wanted them to like her. Since they usually did, she had every reason to expect that Jinx would smile back.

Jinx Kobler did not smile. Her dark eyes were solemn, unfriendly. "What do you want?" she said.

Angie, searching for some shred of an idea, noticed Gold Strike. "I've never met a skunk before. Would he care if I picked him up?"

"How should I know?" Jinx said and walked on.

Angie hesitated a second, then picked the skunk up a bit awkwardly, her hands around his plump little stomach. He offered no objection, but turned his head to grasp her thumb between his teeth. They were sharp teeth, but Gold Strike was only being playful, so she turned her attention back to Jinx. She had her reason for talking to Jinx now, so she caught up with the other girl quickly.

"Maybe you could help me out on something," she began. "Last night your pet here got into our house and I think he took Jasper Junior's toy giraffe. We couldn't find it anywhere this morning, so something must have carried it off. Would you have any idea where Gold Strike might have taken it?"

Jinx stopped again deliberately and looked Angie over very carefully. Then she seemed to make up her mind.

"I know where he'd probably take it," she said. "He's got a special hiding place up there."

Angie looked in the direction Jinx was pointing. The

rock cliff ended before it reached the schoolhouse. The hill above the school rose steeply for a way and then sloped into a stony meadow across which an old mine dump spilled a heap of gray tailings. There were still the remnants of a mill and a wooden shaft house above, but the hill looked precipitous and not at all climbable. In fact, looking at it, you couldn't help wondering why the whole hillside didn't just slide down on top of the school.

"There's a way up," Jinx said. "Come along. Gold Strike, you go on home."

Angie put the skunk down. Jinx clapped her hands at him and he scuttled under the porch steps of the Kobler house.

"He sleeps most of the day," Jinx said, "and roams around at night."

"Doesn't he run away?" Angie asked.

Jinx shook her head. "His mother was killed by a car when he was a baby. He's still not full-grown. He's used to us and he knows we'll feed him. So he always comes home."

Following Jinx, Angie saw that the slope above the road beyond the schoolhouse was rocky, but much less steep. At the foot of the hill was an old building which had probably been a smelter for getting precious metals out of raw ore. Uncle Ben had pointed out other such buildings on their trips. A narrow-gauge rail, now rusty and warped, ran from the building toward the bank of the stream, and a battered ore car lay on its side near the track.

But already Jinx was scrambling up the faint indentation of a path. Before she followed her, Angie stood for a moment looking on ahead through the gap at the lower end of the valley. This was what Uncle Ben had told them about. The narrow wedge of valley opened upon the snow peaks of the Continental Divide, gleaming and beautiful in the distance.

"Oh, look!" Angie breathed. "Just look!"

Jinx followed the direction of her gaze and her expression softened for a moment. Then she said curtly, "Well, are you coming?"

Angie nodded and scrambled after her up the path.
There was no talk between them after that. Jinx's feet
were nimble as any mountain goat's and she was accus-
tomed to the altitude and didn't puff as Angie did. But
Angie did her best to keep up the pace, stopping only
now and then to get her breath and to look down from
the heights on the little gray huddle of Blossom.

"Here we are," Jinx called back and a moment later
she halted among the tumbled rocks on the hillside.
Angie saw the dark hollowing of an entrance to a cave,
saw Jinx disappear through the opening. Since the entrance was only waist-high, Angie dropped down on
her knees to crawl through after Jinx. Inside, the cave
opened into a small cavern. At the rear a tumbling of
rock formed the back of the cave. A faint, cool breath
of air seemed to flow out of the rock pile.

"Gold Strike likes it here," Jinx said. "Sometimes he
comes up to sleep during the day. And he's always hiding things up here."

She knelt on the floor of the cave and put her hand
into a crevice. Then, one by one, she drew out a white
sock, a table napkin, a rubber ball—and Mr. Waldo
Gimmore, not much the worse for his trip up the hill.

"There he is!" Angie cried. "Oh, I'm glad to find
him!"

Jinx held Mr. Gimmore up in the light that filtered
through the cave's entrance. "Seems to me he wouldn't
be much loss if you never found him."

Angie clutched Mr. Gimmore with all the fervor
young Jasper might have displayed, but she had no intention of explaining her affection for the silly old thing
to this unsympathetic girl. Instead she changed the
subject with the first thing that popped into her mind.

"Do you know any place around here that's called
Abednego?" she asked.

"Abednego?" Jinx repeated. "Like in the Bible?
Never heard of anything called that. But Grandpa
would know if anybody does. You can ask him."

"Grandpa?" Angie asked.

"My grandfather," Jinx said, and for the first time

there was a softening in her tone of voice. "He's not home right now. He drove down the mountain for supplies. But he'll be back this afternoon."

"I'll ask him," Angie said, crawling out of the cave. If she didn't get back soon, Mom would be sending a posse of Wetherals out to look for her, just as they'd had to look for Jasper. Anyway, this was one adventure in which she was ahead of Mark. Now she could have the fun of showing him this cave herself.

Jinx came after her and they started down the hill. The other girl seemed no more friendly than before and Angie knew that if it was up to her companion the descent would be made in complete silence. But Angie liked to talk.

"How long have you folks lived in Blossom?" she asked.

"Always," Jinx said.

"Your mother and father too?"

Jinx stopped on the narrow path. "That's none of your business. Nobody asked for you to come snooping around up here. My grandfather was born in that house where we live now. And he was married to Grandmother right here in Blossom. Grandmother used to teach in the schoolhouse down there."

Jinx picked up a handful of pebbles and flung them outward toward the valley. Angie heard them clatter on the sloping roof of the brick schoolhouse far below.

"I didn't mean to make you mad—" Angie began, but Jinx went on fiercely as if she hadn't spoken.

"Now there isn't any more school because there aren't any children to come to it. Nobody works the mines any more. Nobody lives here but us. But we like it in Blossom. We don't want outsiders coming up and snooping. So you leave my mother and father out of it, or I—I'll—" But evidently she couldn't think of any threat terrible enough, so she turned her back and went plunging down the mountainside, leaving Angie to pick her way more cautiously along the trail, both startled and dismayed.

8

"Come Visit Me"

That day the Wetherals put their living quarters into more shipshape condition and Dad got the stovepipe free of nests and debris so that Mom could start the stove. Pitch pine was plentiful and made a good fire. Pine cones substituted nicely for kindling. They located the spring and hauled a water supply across the bridge. Dad set up his portable typewriter in the front bedroom and by midafternoon was pecking away at it. After one look at the sagging shaft house on the hill he had decided that he'd found the ideal place for the book's first murder.

"Thank goodness," Mom said, when he announced his intention. "Now Mr. Guthridge Gilmore will be on the next plane west and we won't have to worry about any more mysteries."

"Mr. Gimmore here," said Jasper, waving the giraffe under his mother's nose.

"Of course, darling," Mom said absently. "Now listen to me, Mark and Angela. I don't want either of you to go near that old mine up on the hillside. Those places are dangerous and not for amateur explorers."

They were all in the living room, catching their breath after a busy day. That is, all except Dad, who was still working at his typewriter in the front bedroom. He heard Mom's words and came to the doorway.

"That's right," he agreed. "No exploring in old

73

mines. I'm going to be pretty careful about looking the place over myself."

Mark grumbled under his breath and made a face at Angie. "Gosh, I'll bet that's just where the treasure is hidden. The one place we can't go."

"What did you say?" Dad asked somewhat sternly. He didn't approve of people who mumbled so that others couldn't hear.

Surprisingly, Mom answered for Mark. "He's afraid the treasure is there. You know—the treasure in that map Uncle Ben gave them."

Angie stared at her mother in amazement and Mark said, "How did you know?"

Mom smiled at them sweetly. "You never give me credit for having any sense. You two have been oozing buried treasure ever since you met Uncle Ben. How could I not know about it?"

"This is beyond me," Dad said in bafflement. "Anyway, you might as well give up any idea of treasure if you got it from Uncle Ben. Every old-timer knows just the place where a million dollars in gold is lying around, if only somebody would dig deep enough. Or he knows the location of a lost mine, if somebody will just give him a grubstake so he can find it. But the easy treasure was taken out of these mountains long ago. So don't let me catch you in any mine tunnels."

He went back to his typewriter and Mom looked sorry about their disappointment, even though she approved the ruling.

"You know what I think would be a nice thing to do?" she said. "Mrs. Kobler pointed out the direction of the Blossom cemetery this morning. So why don't you two pick some wild flowers and take them over to Uncle Ben's grave?"

Angie looked thoughtful, remembering something. "Mom, Uncle Ben said, 'Come visit me.' Do you suppose that's what he meant?"

"Perhaps he did," her mother said. "Anyway, it would be a lovely thing to do. And it will give you a chance to stretch your legs and do some more exploring."

They accepted the suggestion readily enough. There were wild flowers growing along the road—bright pink, lavender, and blue and purple. There was a ferny green plant with tiny yellow blossoms that had a pungent, bitter smell. Angie and Mark gathered a little of everything except the graceful stalks of blue and white columbine. Uncle Ben had told them that was the Colorado state flower and it was against the law to pick it.

As they walked along in the bright light of afternoon they could examine the main street of Blossom more clearly than they had been able to the evening before. The small white church showed more care than the other buildings, and as they passed it they noted that the grass in front had been trimmed and kept free of weeds. Above the door was a scalloped window of stained glass. At least it had once been stained glass. Some of the colored pieces had been replaced with clear window glass. But at least the window was all in one piece.

"Somebody has been taking care of the church," Mark said. "I wonder if that old lady does it? Say— why did you go chasing off after that girl this morning?"

Angie related the adventure she had had in climbing the hillside to recover Mr. Gimmore. There was a grandfather too, she explained, and he was probably the one who took care of the church. Even if they couldn't go exploring the old mine, there was a hillside cave. The treasure might even be hidden in the cave.

"A cave on a hillside isn't at the foot of anything," Mark objected. "This has to be at the foot of something called Abednego, remember?"

"Something which *used* to be there," Angie reminded him. "That makes it a whole lot harder. It's funny, but I had the idea that once we figured out the Blossom part of the map it would be easy to find the place we want. But it seems to be just as hard and far away as ever."

They followed the road across the rickety bridge that was the entrance to town. On the bridge they stood a minute looking up toward the first bend of the winding canyon which the road to town had followed. Blossom Creek poured down out of that canyon, fed by watersheds and gulches which cut the canyon's sides. Then they struck off up an overgrown path on the far hillside in the direction Mrs. Kobler had pointed out. With two turns of the path Blossom was behind them and they were alone with the mountains and quiet groves.

They found the cemetery by accident when Angie stumbled over a broken headstone and they became aware of other markers around them. There were pine trees everywhere and a grove of aspens had grown up in the neglected plots, their slender trunks looking like birch, except for the greenish-white color. Over the entire scene lay a sleeping peace. Beyond the little aspen grove a mountain sloped gracefully, dark with pine, serene and beautiful. In the distance was the now familiar sound of rushing water.

The graves seemed to follow no orderly pattern. Here and there a retaining wall of rock had been built to level the ground and keep the hillside from washing away.

Angie paused to scan a weathered stone that read, "Born in Wales in 1820." Her feet slipped on the heavy matting of cones and pine needles and she began to wonder how they would ever find Uncle Ben's grave in this wandering place.

It was Mark who first saw the old man sitting on the hillside below them. He had white hair, but, unlike Uncle Ben, he wore no beard. He looked up at them calmly, watching their approach. They stopped uncertainly. This, Angie decided, must be Jinx's grandfather, but after the unfriendly welcome the rest of the family had given them, she hesitated to speak first.

"You looking for Ben Ellington's grave?" the old man asked.

He didn't sound unfriendly and Angie slid down the brown needles of the slope until she was near him.

Mark came down more slowly, always less ready to make friends with a stranger.

"That's right," Angie said. "We brought these," and she held up her bouquet of flowers.

The old man looked at the blossoms approvingly. "A good mountain choice, young lady. Those pinkish flowers are bouncing Bet, and the ferny stuff is good, old-fashioned tansy. Up here we call its little yellow flowers 'bitter buttons.' Ben Ellington would like you bringing him these. You can put 'em over here if you want."

He motioned to a low mound beside him where the surface of the earth had been turned and left uncovered by the pine needles which blanketed the rest of the area. Angie saw that faded flowers had been neatly cleared from the mound and that an old peanut butter jar held fresh blooms. There was still room for hers in the jar and she thrust their thirsty stems down into the water.

"Set down awhile," the old man invited and they dropped down on the springy brown needles beside him. "Let's see now—you'd be Mark and Angela Wetheral. My granddaughter told me about you when I got back from town this afternoon."

"So you must be Mr. Kobler," Angie said.

He nodded without putting his answer into words, and they sat for a while in the peaceful quiet, with only the wind pushing past the pines to set aspen leaves aquiver. When the round leaves trembled and shimmered they looked like silver dollars, Angie thought.

An appreciative smile broke through Grandpa Kobler's wrinkles. "The quakers are having a fine dance for themselves, aren't they?"

"Quakers?" Mark said, still holding back uncertainly.

The old man nodded, and his soft white hair lifted gently as the wind touched it. "That's mountain talk, boy. It's what we call the quaking aspens."

"You sound like Uncle Ben," Angie said.

"I take that as a fine compliment, Angela," he said. "There's nobody living or dead I'd rather be like than

Ben Ellington. We were friends from 'way back, though he was ten years older. I was a kid when he moved in and practically bought the town. Later I had a general store down on the main street. I've seen Ben Ellington through good times and bad times. The last years he spent in Blossom were pretty hard."

"How do you mean?" Mark asked.

"Well—that was before his wife and baby died. Afterward the place never seemed right to him again, so he moved down to Boulder and said he wouldn't come back to stay till he came here for good—the way he has now."

"We didn't know about his wife and baby," Angie said softly.

Mr. Kobler got to his feet with a bit of a heave. Though he wasn't as old as Uncle Ben, he moved more slowly and painfully. "Look over here," he said.

Following him around the foot of Uncle Ben's grave, they saw two other graves beyond. One was heartbreakingly tiny and there was a small silver plaque with lettering on it: "OUR DARLING." Angie felt a lump rise in her throat and Mark blinked and looked off at the opposite mountainside.

"Diphtheria," Mr. Kobler said. "It took an awful lot of folks in the mining days. That little girl used to play right out in the yard of the house where you're staying now. That was Ben's place when times got bad and he couldn't keep up his big house in Denver."

"But wasn't there—" Mark began and then hesitated, seeking the right words. "Wasn't there something valuable up here that would have helped him through bad times? I mean some kind of treasure?"

Mr. Kobler's smile was mild. "Well now, boy, that's what you might call a moot question. If there was anything of the sort, it didn't come to light while his family was alive. I know in later years he got some kind of bee in his bonnet. Once he asked me right out if I'd like a fortune handed to me."

"What did you say?" Mark asked eagerly.

Mr. Kobler winked at him slyly. "You think I'd

want that woman of mine getting me down to Denver where I'd have to dress up in boiled shirts and crook my little finger at tea parties? Me—who was born in the mountains when Blossom was a boom town! I told him to run along with his fortunes. I'd seen too much of what a whole lot of money could do to men—and women too, for that matter. That's the way he felt himself. It came too late for him, if there *was* a treasure. By that time he didn't want any part of it, either."

This was beyond Mark's understanding. "I don't see why anybody wouldn't want to find treasure if it was right there."

"Well now, Ben got the idea that if it hadn't been for getting rich too easy in the first place, maybe he'd have been a different kind of man. Maybe he'd have made a decent, ordinary living, and he'd never have had to bring his family up here to Blossom where diphtheria took them."

"But they could have caught that anywhere," Angie said.

"That's what I used to tell him. And I used to remind him that he and his wife spent some happy years up here. But he blamed himself, and it got so he was a little touched on the subject of easy money. He wouldn't give a quarter to anybody who didn't work for it."

"But he offered the—the treasure to you," Mark said.

"I guess he thought I was a hard worker anyway and it wouldn't go to my head. But I didn't want it. I had plenty in those days. My wife had plans to send our son down to Denver to college and there was enough for that. When it didn't get used, I put it into one of Ben's silver mines and it got wiped out in a crash. But even then I didn't care much. We had what we wanted. Ben's always paid me something to come up here summers and look after things so the whole town wouldn't just blow away, like some towns have done."

The old man seemed to be musing half to himself. Angie waited for him to go on.

"Real treasure's only found inside a man, after all. If he's got that kind, what he digs out of the ground don't matter so much. If he don't have it, the stuff out of the ground won't make him happy anyway. But I remember Ben said once that he was going to make it plenty hard for anybody to find that treasure he knew about."

"He sure has," Mark said.

Grandpa Kobler's eyes twinkled and he aimed a sudden question at Angie. "You're about my granddaughter's age, Angela—what do you think of her?"

Angie picked up a pine cone and broke off the brown segments with great concentration. How could she tell Jinx's grandfather that she thought the girl strange and unfriendly?

The old man had his answer from her silence.

"That's what I suspected," he said. "Pretty sharp with you, wasn't she?"

"Well," Angie tossed the cone away, "she doesn't want us here. She said Blossom was just for you folks and she didn't like outsiders coming in."

"She's turning into a little Rocky Mountain critter," Grandpa Kobler said. "We go down the mountain to live in winters, but school doesn't seem to tame her much. Anyway, it's just another mountain school. Maybe she needs something different. Sometimes I get to thinking about that treasure Ben used to hint about. Maybe I ought to take a look around and see if there's anything to it just for her sake."

Mark wriggled uneasily. "We're looking for it too. We need a fortune real bad."

"Oh, Mark!" Angie said. "We don't need a *fortune*. We'd just like to get enough ahead so Dad could have time to write his novel, instead of doing those old mysteries all the time. Anyway, even with the map Uncle Ben gave us, we don't know where to look for it."

Grandpa Kobler's eyes twinkled. "I've heard about those maps Ben used to give out. He even offered me one once, but I didn't take it."

"We've got everything figured out," Mark said, "except where and what Abednego is."

"Abednego?" Grandpa Kobler repeated.

Angie looked at him eagerly. "Yes! That's a word on the map. The treasure is supposed to be at the foot of something called Abednego. Jinx said you might know what it is."

But Mr. Kobler shook his head. " 'Fraid I don't. It sounds familiar somehow—like I'd heard it someplace before. But I don't seem to pin it down to anything I can remember."

He stood up, moving in the same slow, painful way Angie had noted before. "Not as spry as I used to be," he said. "Well, I guess I'd better be getting along home. Mother likes supper on time and the sun's getting low. Did my granddaughter tell you that Miz Kobler came up here to teach in the Blossom school? Pretty little stiff-necked thing she was in those days, with lots of spunk. If only she didn't take that word 'duty' so hard!"

He sighed and started back through the aspen grove toward the path. Angie and Mark followed him, Angie still seething with questions she didn't know how to ask. What had happened to his son that the college money was never used? Who was Jinx's mother, and where was she? But now Grandpa Kobler walked along in silence, his thoughts far away as if he hardly noticed his two young companions.

Not till they were back in town opposite the church did he speak again. "I don't know what your religion is, but God's the same anyplace, so maybe you folks would like to join us over here tomorrow morning? I'm no preacher, so there's no service, rightly speaking. But we read the Bible for a little while and then we just sit in there quiet-like and think our thoughts so God can hear 'em. Suppose you ask your mother and father."

"I'm sure they'd like to come," Angie said quickly. "Could you stop in and meet them now?"

He shook his head. "No time. But you bring 'em over in the morning, if they'd like to come." He paused and looked at her for a moment thoughtfully. "Another thing, Angela—do you suppose you could bear with

Juanita for a spell? I mean, don't heed her sharp ways. She needs a friend real bad. Another girl her own age."

"Juanita?" Angie repeated wonderingly.

"That's her real name. It's the one I like to call her by."

"It's a very pretty name," Angie said.

The old man touched her shoulder lightly with his hand. "Suppose you tell her that sometime."

He went off down the road. Mark stared after him. "If that's her name, why do they call her Jinx?" he said. "I don't get it."

"I don't either," Angie agreed.

She went into the house wondering about the request Grandpa Kobler had made of her. How did you get to be friends with someone who didn't want to be friends with you? And how had the girl been given a name like Juanita?

9

The Room
in the Tower

That evening the Wetherals ate a hot supper of canned hamburgers and spaghetti, which Mom had been able to heat on top of the stove. There was a salad too, made from lettuce and tomatoes they'd brought with them, and the last of some cake that was getting stale.

Angie, still thinking about the name Juanita, brought up the subject while they ate.

"That's a Spanish name," Dad said. "And your Jinx looks as if there was Spanish or Mexican blood in her background. She has the dark eyes and skin and the black hair."

"There's probably a romantic story there," Mom mused dreamily, renewing Mark's plateful of spaghetti. "Perhaps she'll tell you sometime."

Angie shook her head. "She acted as though I'd insulted her when I asked about her mother and father. She certainly is a funny sort of girl."

"You might be too if you'd had her raising," Mom said. "Anyway, I think it's lovely of Mr. Kobler to ask us over to the church tomorrow morning. I'm looking forward to that."

They all slept quietly that night. No small black and white animal prowled the house, no banshee wails interrupted the normal mountain-night sounds, and Mr. Gimmore was found safely under Jasper's bed in the morning.

They were all tired enough to sleep late, so there was much hurrying into clean jeans and shirts, which was the best they could manage for church, since Mom hadn't expected them to need dress-up clothes in a ghost town.

The morning was sparkling clear, and the distant snow peaks of the Divide shone white in the sun. The stream that rushed through Blossom seemed livelier than ever as it leaped over rocks and broke into rainbow spray in its hurry to get down to the plains.

The Koblers were sitting on the sagging wooden steps of the church waiting for them. The old man shook hands cordially with Dad and Mom and made friends at once with young Jasper. Mrs. Kobler was polite, but stiff, and she didn't put herself out to respond to Mom's friendly attempts at conversation. Jinx watched the Wetherals with dark suspicion, never smiling at all. Mark reacted to this by turning prickly himself. He didn't like Jinx and he didn't care who knew it.

Probably the little church had never seen an odder congregation. When she went through the door, Angie stopped a moment to look around. The walls were natural wood and there were beautiful weathered old beams supporting the roof. The wooden pews were polished from long use and there was no carpet covering the worn boards of the aisle. The altar was as plain and simple as the front of a schoolroom, except for the little raised platform on which the lectern stood.

Mrs. Kobler and Jinx went at once to a bench on the left-hand side, as if it were the place they always took. After a moment's hesitation Mom chose the opposite pew on the right. "To spread out the congregation," she whispered to Dad. Mark followed her, but Angie hung back and slipped into place next to Jinx, giving her a quick, curious glance as she did so. Jinx stared straight ahead and paid no more attention than if Angie had been thin air.

They had lowered their voices as they came in and there was a hush now in the small church as Grandpa

Kobler went slowly up to the lectern and placed a leather-bound Bible upon it. Behind them, the window over the door filtered sunlight through in a pattern of shadow and colored light. Even Jasper understood that now was the time for quiet and, though he wriggled a little, he did not chatter but hugged Mr. Gimmore to him in silence.

As they watched Grandpa Kobler's wrinkled hands turning the thin pages of the Bible, Angie became aware for the first time of the beauty of the lectern itself. The handsome grain of the wood had been rubbed to a soft, smoky brown. Someone must have spent long hours building it and then bringing out the satiny luster of the wood.

Grandpa Kobler addressed himself first to the Wetherals, welcoming them to Blossom in a simple way that made Angie feel that he was truly glad they were here. Then he read them a verse from the One Hundred and Third Psalm:

" 'The wind passeth over it, and it is gone;
And the place thereof shall know it no more.' "

He meant the little mountain town of Blossom, over which the great hot wind of the gold fever had passed. The wind was gone now, and Blossom, sleeping peacefully in its narrow wedge of valley, with old mine scars on the hills above, would know that wind no more. He told them simply about the life of Blossom, and by his tone you knew he loved this place and was sad because it was only a matter of years before it would be, like other towns, a few rotting timbers lost in sage and mountain grass. It rested now in its old age, but he thought the town must be pleased that once more young feet trod its paths and young eyes explored its secrets.

Then he read again from the Bible.

When he closed the black leather covers, his hands strayed from them momentarily and moved with love over the smooth, polished wood of the lectern. Then he came down from the little platform and sat beside Angie and bowed his head. This was the time he had meant when he said they would be quiet and let God hear their thoughts.

There was no man-made organ music here, but Angie heard the soft sighing of the pines and the singing of birds and she had a sense of being very close to a great and comforting Presence.

Afterward, as they walked along the main street of Blossom, with Jasper squealing and running to make up for being so quiet, Mrs. Kobler, who had not said more than three words to anyone, suddenly turned to Mrs. Wetheral.

"We'd be proud to have you come for Sunday dinner," she said stiffly. "We eat around one o'clock. Nothing fancy in the way of cooking, but we'd be pleased to have your company."

Mom and Dad thanked her warmly, and Angie glanced at Jinx to see what the other girl's reaction to this invitation might be. But Jinx had not changed her expression. It was plain that she, at least, was not looking forward to company for dinner this Sunday.

Before dinner there was time for Angie to take Mark up the hill to show him Gold Strike's cave. The skunk had been there again because a red hair ribbon which probably belonged to Jinx had been tucked into the crevice of rock where Gold Strike kept his treasures. It was in a slightly chewed condition, but Angie tucked it in her pocket to return to its owner.

Mark poked around the cave and stirred up the rubble of fallen rock at the back, but revealed nothing of interest. There were no signs of what might, according to Mark, be a gold vein.

When they climbed downhill again and went home, Mom set them to work clipping a few sprays and small branches from the giant blue spruce in the yard. She set these in an old-fashioned gold and white china water pitcher she had found among the things in the locked-up room. Set on a table in the living room, the pitcher, with its spreading branches of spruce, dressed things up and made the room seem less bare. It brought the wonderful spruce smell inside too, to counteract occasional smoky puffs from the little stove in the back room.

Just before one o'clock they set off down the road to the Koblers' house. Mark was fascinated by the little dome effect of the cupola above the front porch.

"That's the kind of room I'd like to have," he said. "You could see all over the whole valley. You could see anybody who came down the road."

"That's probably how Jinx saw us the day we arrived," Angie said.

Mrs. Kobler had a gas range in her kitchen, as well as a small wood-burning stove, and kept a supply of bottled gas on hand, both to light the house and to cook with. Angie sniffed hungrily the wonderful cooking odors the minute she entered the house and Mark said, "Mm-mmm," dreamily.

Mrs. Kobler was busy in the kitchen and came out just long enough to greet them. Jinx was helping bring food into the dining room and spoke only a grudging, "Hello." But Grandpa was so cordial and hospitable that you'd have thought he entertained ghost town visitors every day of the week.

The living room and dining room were furnished in an old-fashioned way which delighted Mom, though Angie couldn't help thinking that there were too many doodads and that the furniture had a heavy, dark look, as if it were intended to be more impressive than comfortable.

On the sideboard in the dining room Mark discovered a beautiful little bird made of polished wood, with its wings spread as if it were about to fly away. Mark loved craft work, and he picked it up admiringly, stroking his fingers over the smooth, shinning wood.

Grandpa Kobler noticed his interest. "Like it?" he asked.

Mark nodded. "It's awfully pretty. And I like the way it feels too."

"Grandpa made it," Jinx put in, and Angie caught a note of pride in her voice. "We go out in the mountains looking for old pieces of pitch pine and limber pine, and aspen and cedar and most anything. Just so it has an interesting shape. Grandpa can always see the birds and animals, and people and things, that are hidden in the wood."

"Dinner's ready," Mrs. Kobler announced abruptly, and they all sat down at the table.

There was even a high chair for Jasper—one that had belonged to Jinx as a baby. They had to tear him away from Gold Strike to put him into it. Mom had tried to explain that daytime was a skunk's time for sleeping, but Jasper had prodded him awake and Gold Strike had been playing with him drowsily.

When he'd said grace, Grandpa Kobler began dishing up hearty servings from a huge bowl set before him.

"Our Cousin Jenny here," he said, smiling at Grandmother Kobler, "has cooked us up a real sowbelly dinner. Bet you've never tasted anything so good."

"Cousin Jenny?" Mom asked.

Grandmother Kobler explained in her stiff way. "In the early days a lot of people came over from Cornwall in England to work the mines. Everybody called the Cornish folk Cousin Jacks and Cousin Jennys. That's what my people were—Cornish."

The sowbelly dinner was as delicious as Grandpa Kobler claimed. There was salt pork in it, and potatoes, and navy beans, all cooked together for hours into a savory stew. On the side there was cabbage with sour-cream dressing, onions sliced in vinegar, cold red tomatoes, and tall glasses of creamy milk. Mrs. Kobler explained that she had a little garden out in back of the house, though it was hard to raise things in mountain soil. And there was an old cow up on a higher meadow, who still gave good, rich milk.

Even while he filled his mouth with Mrs. Kobler's wonderful food, Mark could not take his eyes from other wood pieces of Grandpa Kobler's which stood on shelves about the dining room. When there was a pause in the grown-up conversation—mostly between Dad and Mom and Grandpa Kobler—Mark edged over to Grandpa, who sat next to him at the table.

"Do you think I could make one of these birds or something if I found a piece of pine? Could you show me how?"

"I'd be glad to, young man," Grandpa Kobler said. "You come over and see me tomorrow morning and I'll take you through my workshop."

"There's a store in Denver that buys everything Grandpa sends them," Jinx said proudly. She seemed willing enough to come out of her shell when she could talk about her grandfather. You could see her love for him showing in her eyes, hear it in the tone of her voice. If only, Angie thought, Jinx wouldn't be so prickly when it came to everyone else!

After dinner Mom insisted that they were neighbors and nothing would do but she must help Mrs. Kobler with the dishes. Dad settled down on the shady side veranda for a talk with Grandpa, while Mark got to another subject that interested him.

"What's up in that tower room over the front porch?" he asked Jinx.

"That's my room," said Jinx curtly.

"Gosh!" Mark said, "I'd sure like to look out that window."

"No reason why you can't," Mrs. Kobler spoke from the dining room where she was clearing off the table. "Jinx, take your company upstairs and show them your room."

Jinx looked at her grandmother darkly, and there was rebellion in the set of her lower lip. Angie tried to think of some way to change the subject and make Mark forget about the room, but it was too late. Jinx was going to refuse and Angie squirmed uncomfortably. She hated to have people get angry with one another and make unpleasant scenes. But Grandpa Kobler had heard from his place on the veranda outside the dining room window and he broke in.

"Juanita—" he began.

"I don't want anybody else in my room," Jinx said heatedly.

Mrs. Kobler opened her mouth, but Grandpa spoke first. "When a fellow has something special that's nicer than what somebody else has, he ought to be willing to share, Juanita. He ought to be kind to them that in some ways has less."

Jinx stared at him, puzzled.

"After all," her grandfather went on, "you've got a room in a tower. Now not very many folks have any such, and Mark wants to see it. You've got a room with a view of one of the nicest little valleys in the mountains. Don't you want to share that when you get a chance?"

"We'd love to see it," Angie said warmly, wanting to help Grandpa Kobler. "All we ever see back in New York is concrete and sidewalks and other people's windows."

Jinx shifted her dark gaze to Angie's face for a moment. Then she turned on her heel and walked toward the stairs. "Come on, then, if you want to. But I'm only doing it for Grandpa."

She thumped her way ahead of them up the dark stairway. The hall above was equally dark until she flung open a door at the front of the house and walked ahead of them into her room.

Compared to Angie's room at home, this was a bare, unbeautiful little place. The furniture was old and battered and there wasn't much of it. But the room was tidy and very clean. On the dresser was a lovely little fawn shape that Grandpa Kobler had dreamed into a piece of wood.

Mark, however, went straight to the tower part of the room and looked out one of the windows. He whistled over the view.

"You could sit here and read and then just look up and see the mountains," he said. "The stream is real close here too so you can hear it singing, even though it's around in back."

Angie stood behind her brother, looking out the win-

dows in the tower. Through one she could see clear to
the blue slopes and white points of the snow peaks.
Through another she could see Blossom's main street
and the gray little buildings of the town, with the sheer
rock mountain rising above. She could see their own
house quite plainly, with the tall blue spruce tree raising its graceful branches above.

"Were you watching us from this window when we
arrived in Blossom?" Angie asked Jinx.

The other girl stood behind them, still obviously
afraid that they meant to make fun of her.

"Yes," Jinx said, "that's where I watched you. I can
see just about everything that happens in Blossom from
that window."

"And later you came down and watched us through
the jail window, didn't you?" Mark said.

Jinx nodded. "Why shouldn't I?"

"Oh, no reason," Angie said hastily. "Say—maybe
you can tell us why the doors of that room at Uncle
Ben's house were bolted shut from the inside, when the
back door was gone completely."

Jinx explained willingly enough. "The back door was
falling apart, so Grandpa took it off the hinges just a
few days ago to repair it. I bolted those doors and
climbed out the back way. It just made it a little harder
for any strangers who broke in the front of the house
to get at the furniture."

Mark gave a little snort of disgust. "That's the trouble with mysteries! In the end they always turn out to
be something simple after all."

Angie, looking out a window over Mark's shoulder,
could see the jail and the funny little firehouse. She
could see the bandstand, and clear to where the road
turned to cross the bridge. She could even see the tall
man who was coming down the road, carrying a knapsack of some sort on his back.

"My goodness!" Angie cried. "There's somebody else
coming into Blossom!"

Jinx came to see, and the three stared down the road
for a moment.

"Let's go find out who he is and what he wants," Mark suggested. "After all, we don't want a lot of strangers snooping around Blossom."

Jinx gave him a startled look, and then glanced at Angie. Angie laughed out loud and Jinx let her solemn mouth slip into a momentary smile over the way Mark sounded as if he'd lived here always. Mark, paying no attention to the girls, started downstairs and they hurried after him.

The three approached the man just as he came opposite the ramshackle stores. He saw them coming and eased his big knapsack down onto the wooden sidewalk, set the small blue metal box he was carrying beside it, and waited for them.

Angie saw that he was young and rather tall and thin. His face was sunburned to a bright pink and he wore glasses with dark rims. He grinned as they came up to him.

"Hi, kids! I take it this is the town of Blossom?"

Since Jinx said nothing, Angie answered. "Yes, it is."

"That's fine," said the young man. "My name's Bill Rolfe and I've come up here from Boulder. Got a lift part way, but had to walk the last few miles. Whew! That Colorado sun sure can get hot!"

Jinx found her tongue. "What do you want here?" she demanded.

Bill Rolfe seemed not to mind her abrupt manner. He mopped his face with an amazingly patterned handkerchief of green, blue, yellow, and orange. "That's a fair enough question. But first let me ask you one of my own. Do you kids know, or have you ever heard of any place, or thing, or whatever, around this town called Abednego?"

10

Shaft House

Angie looked at Mark in dismay and Jinx said, "What *is* this Abednego that everybody's so interested in?"

Bill Rolfe did not answer. He was staring in horror down the road beyond them, as if all the ghosts of Blossom were stalking toward him.

"R-r-run for your life!" he cried in a strangled voice and took off in the direction from which he had come, his feet throwing up little puffs of dust behind him.

Angie looked around in alarm to see what had frightened him.

"It's only Gold Strike," Jinx said disgustedly. "Everybody's scared of him."

Sure enough, the little skunk was trotting down the road toward them with his peculiar rolling gait, his bushy plume of a tail waving aloft. Evidently he had wearied of Jasper's attentions and, since his nap had been spoiled anyway, he had come out to see what was happening in the world. Angie bent to hold out her hands and the little fellow trotted over to her fearlessly. She clasped him around his plump little body, feeling the coarse bristly hair under her fingers, and lifted him to her shoulder. He balanced there as if on familiar territory, while they all started out to rescue Bill Rolfe.

The young man had disappeared entirely from view, but now he put his head around the side of the jail and watched them, openmouthed.

"It's all right," Angie assured him. "Come on out. Gold Strike won't hurt you. He's a pet."

He came out a bit sheepishly and had a closer look at the skunk. Then he remembered something and hurried to where he had left his baggage. He picked up the blue metal box and looked it over carefully.

"None of you kids touched this, did you?" he demanded.

They shook their heads and he tucked it under his arm in evident relief. "Well, don't ever. Just remember that."

"Just don't you touch any of our things," Jinx told him tartly.

Bill Rolfe grinned at her. "Guess I did sound sort of bossy. Well, this little contraption cost me plenty and I wouldn't want anything to happen to it."

"What is it?" Angie asked, pushing Gold Strike's black little nose out of her neck.

Bill didn't answer, but looked around him curiously. "Do you kids know if there's a hotel in this town?"

That struck Angie and Mark as hilarious and even Jinx smiled.

Bill didn't mind being laughed at. "Well, then, do you know whether one of these houses is in good enough shape to camp in?"

Jinx nodded in the direction of the jail. "That's the best built place in town. If you don't mind sleeping in a cell. But what if we don't want you to stay here?"

He paid no attention, but crossed the road to the jail, pulled the door open, and disappeared inside. A moment later he looked out at them from behind one of the barred windows.

"How's about helping me move in?" he called.

Jinx said, "Why should we?" to Angie, but Mark waved a finger, hushing her.

"We don't want him here, but we've got to find out what he knows about Abednego."

"Why?" said Jinx. "What do I care about your old Abednego? Nobody can put you out of Blossom be-

cause Uncle Ben left you that house. But *he* doesn't belong here."

Bill's face had disappeared from the window and
they could hear him banging around inside the jail.

"He's bigger than I am," Mark said. "I'm not going
to try to put him out."

Angie set Gold Strike down on the road. He really
wasn't a very cuddly pet. He always wanted to pull
your hair or chew on an ear.

"Me either," said Angie. "Let's go see what he
wants."

She and Mark looked in the door and saw that Bill
was pulling old cartons, dented pans, and wooden
boxes out of one of the cells. He glanced at them cheerfully over one shoulder.

"It won't be half bad, when I clear out some of the
junk. Well now—would you look at this!"

The cell was lost in gloom, but when he turned
around, Angie could see that he held a basket of rocks
in his hands.

"Ore specimens," Mark said. "Like Uncle Ben had."

Bill nodded. "I know. My subject at the university is
geology. This might be an interesting find. Who's Uncle
Ben?"

Angie and Mark looked at each other, and Angie
knew her brother's eyebrow was cautioning her—just
the way Dad did sometimes with Mom.

"Why are you looking for something called Abednego?" Mark countered.

Bill Rolfe took his glasses off, held them up to the
light, his brown eyes squinting against the glare, and
began to polish them carefully with his gaudy handkerchief. Angie suspected that he was trying to think up a
good answer that wouldn't tell them everything. She
saw no reason for being cautious herself. If he knew
about Abednego, then he knew about the treasure.

"Do you have a map?" she asked straight out.

He hooked the tortoise shell stems over his ears and
peered at her through the newly polished lenses. "A
map?" he echoed innocently.

"Probably you have one of those maps Uncle Ben gave out all over the place," Angie went on, ignoring a dig in the ribs from Mark's elbow. "The one with Abednego on it."

Bill Rolfe seemed to come to a decision. He unbuttoned the pocket of his zipper jacket and took out a folded sheet of paper.

"Is this what you mean by a map? I got this from a ranger down in Boulder. I really don't know your Uncle Ben."

Mark gave up being cautious. "That's Sam Springer. He told us about giving away his map. But we have one too. And we're looking for Abednego."

"Well!" Bill whistled, and then grinned at them. "Looks like the gold-rush days are here again. Whoever finds color first—well, finders keepers. First come, first served."

That was all right, Angie thought. If this Bill Rolfe wanted to think the treasure was gold, let him. Maybe he hadn't figured out the black diamonds part of the map.

He started to fold up the sheet of paper, but Jinx, who had been listening alertly, suddenly held out her hand.

"Let me see," she said.

He hesitated a moment, looking at her dark, intent little face with the curly tendrils of black hair framing it where they had escaped the tight braids. Then he handed over the map and waited to see what she would say.

Jinx examined it from all angles before she gave it back to him. "What does it mean?"

"It's supposed to mean treasure," Bill said. "Treasure buried at the foot of something called Abednego."

"Treasure?" Jinx repeated. "Here in Blossom?"

Both Angie and Bill nodded.

"Then you won't find it!" Jinx told them, her voice suddenly sharp. "You'll never find it!"

"O.K.," Bill said pleasantly. "Now do you suppose one of you two young ladies could get me a broom? I want to clean out my hotel room so I can move into it tonight."

"I'll get you a broom," Angie said, and started off down the road.

Jinx was after her at once, scuffing along beside her in the dust. "Do you really think there's treasure buried around here?"

"I don't know," Angie said. "We wouldn't know where to look anyway—not without finding out about Abednego. But what did you mean when you told that Bill Rolfe that he'd never find it?"

"You never will either." Jinx tossed her head defiantly, and the heavy braids bounced against her back.

Why Jinx should make such a statement, Angie didn't know, but now they'd reached the Wetheral house and she hurried toward the door.

"I'm going to get a broom," she said, and left Jinx in the yard.

She found a broom in the kitchen, but when she returned to the front of the house, Mark was standing in the road, watching Bill Rolfe stalk off in the direction of the schoolhouse, with Jinx trailing him a few yards behind.

"Where's he going?" Angie asked. "I thought he wanted a broom."

Mark pointed at the mountainside above the school. "He saw that old shaft house up there and he said that meant a mine. So he lost interest in cleaning out the jail and started off to find the way up. He took that blue box with him, as if somebody might steal it if he left it behind. I guess Jinx means to trail him."

"I'm going too," Angie said. "You want to come?"

Mark fell into step beside her on the road, but at the moment he had no further interest in Bill Rolfe. "Mrs. Kobler said I could have another piece of apple pie when the last one jogged down, so I'm going back for that. Dad said to stay away from that mine anyway, so you can't go up there."

"We can watch him," Angie said and hurried after Jinx, leaving Gold Strike to follow Mark back to the

Koblers'. Overhead a black cloud was edging over the sun and she wondered if a shower was due.

Jinx gave no sign of pleasure at Angie's company. She merely accepted it. Bill Rolfe didn't seem to mind being trailed. He looked back at them once or twice and even waved, as if he were just taking a casual walk in the hills. But it was evident that he had a strong interest in the mill and the old shaft house, propped crazily on the mountainside.

The huge dump from the mine cut off any direct ascent, but Bill stopped at the edge of it and kicked at the rocks with one foot. Then he began to skirt the dump, climbing nearer the shaft house.

Jinx increased her speed and Angie, puffing after her, sensed the other girl's anxiety.

"What's the matter?" Angie asked. "What are you worried about?"

"I'm not worried," Jinx denied. "What do I care what happens to him?" But she hurried nevertheless, her feet slipping on the stones in her haste.

The tilting gray timbers of the shaft house were directly above them now. The long roof slanted downhill into a bin. The back stood flat against the hillside. But Bill was heading for the doorway of the shaft house. Jinx stopped and cupped her hands around her mouth to give her voice carrying force.

"Hey, you!" she called. "Hey, you—Bill Rolfe!"

He stopped beside the rotting timbers and looked down at the two girls. The sun shone on his glasses so they couldn't see his eyes, but to Angie his mouth seemed to have lost its friendly grin. Bill Rolfe, she suspected, was beginning to be annoyed.

"Now what do you want?" he asked.

They scrambled up to his level, and Angie found herself looking with both interest and doubt at the tumble-down hoist room which hid the entrance to the shaft. She supposed it was all right, so long as she didn't go inside. Mom hadn't said she couldn't look at the outside.

"You can't go in there," Jinx cried, and Angie heard the odd quaver in her voice.

"Now look here, you two." Bill folded his arms in a gesture that indicated he was exerting more patience than he felt. "I didn't ask for your charming company on this little mountain climb. I'm not asking you to tell me what I may or may not do. Will you just be good little girls and go back to Blossom and play with your dolls?"

Jinx ignored the insult. Her small brown hands were clenched so tightly into fists that the skin stretched shiny across the knuckles.

"I'm telling you," she said. "Don't go inside that mine!"

For answer Bill turned on his heel and went through the rickety door. Jinx stared after him for a moment with very real fright in her eyes. Then to Angie's amazement she whirled around and started down the dump with reckless haste. Before she had gone twenty feet, with Angie behind her, now a little frightened herself because of the contagion of fear, the rain came down. In the Colorado manner sudden buckets were tipped out of a boiling black cloud, while a mountain peak away the sky was still blue. Jinx changed her course and scurried like a chipmunk for the shelter of Gold Strike's cave on the hillside. Angie followed her, stumbling and sliding, drenched to the skin, her teeth chattering with the sudden cold.

The cave was dry shelter, and warm except for the cool draft of air that seemed to blow out from behind the tumbled rocks at the back. Angie huddled down on the rock floor, patting water from her jeans, wiping her face with a quickly sodden handkerchief. Jinx made no effort to dry herself, but crouched beside Angie, peering out at the flooding sheets of rain. But she didn't seem to see the rain. In her eyes lurked the remembrance of something frightening and painful.

"Why are you afraid of that mine?" Angie asked softly. "Why did you run away?"

For once Jinx did not scowl at her, or thrust away her interest. She drew back into the cave, shivering.

"My father was the last person who ever went into that mine. The last, that is, except for the men who brought him out. He was killed in a rock fall. Grandpa doesn't let anybody go in there any more." .

Angie caught her breath, but she could find no words that seemed right to speak, so she reached out and touched Jinx's arm sympathetically with her cold fingers. Jinx drew back from her touch, rejecting her sympathy. The moment of hurt had passed and she was her usual defiant self.

"If there's treasure in that mine you'll never get it out. Never! Grandpa will stop you. He'll stop that Bill Rolfe too, if he doesn't get himself killed first. My father thought there was still a fortune down there— though people who knew said there wasn't. He wouldn't listen to Grandpa and he went down anyway."

Jinx crawled to the entrance and put her head out into the rain so she could look up toward the shaft house on the hill above. Then she ducked back out of the wet and Angie saw the relief on her face.

"He's all right," Jinx said. "He's standing there in the door waiting for the rain to stop. What's he got in that blue box? His lunch?"

Angie wasn't interested in the box. "Do you remember your father, Jinx?"

"The accident happened when I was very small," Jinx said.

"And your mother—what about her?"

For the first time Jinx seemed ready to release into words some of the hurt pent up inside her. "She died a little while afterward of pneumonia. Grandpa says she didn't take any interest in living after what happened to my father. But Grandmother says he should never have married her in the first place."

"Why not?"

"He gave up his college work, everything to make a home for them. Grandmother said he might have been a great scientist. That's why she hated my mother. Because of that and because my mother was a Mexican girl. That's why she hates me too."

Angie wriggled uncomfortably. This sudden shocking storm from Jinx made her want to put her hands over her ears and not listen any more. "Your very own grandmother couldn't hate you," she protested weakly.

Jinx laughed, but the sound was not a happy one. "That's what you think. She's only raising me because it's her duty. She even hates my name because my mother chose it for me."

"I think Juanita's a pretty name," Angie said gently.

Jinx almost snapped at her. "I don't like it. When I was little and Grandmother wanted to scold me she called me a little jinx. So I took that for my name. And now I'm glad I did. I don't *want* to be half Mexican. I want to be a hundred per cent American."

"Your grandfather calls you Juanita."

"I can't stop *him*," Jinx said.

Thunder clapped outside and a tongue of lightning ran along a distant peak far beyond their valley.

Angie clapped her hands over her ears, forgetting everything but the storm.

Jinx gave her a quick look of scorn. "You're not afraid of this, are you? The lightning's a long way off. You can tell by the wait before the thunder. Just so the rain lets up before it starts something, there's nothing to be afraid of."

Angie uncovered her ears. "Starts something? What do you mean?"

"Ever seen a gully washer—a flash flood?"

"No," Angie said. "What is it?"

"A twenty-foot, or maybe fifty-foot, wall of water can come tearing down one of these canyons and wipe out a town before you know what's coming. I've seen places where it's happened. A pretty little stream like Blossom Creek can be turned into a mud flat and whole mountainsides can cave in."

"Could that happen around here?" Angie asked, dismayed.

"My grandfather says it did happen once—before there was any town of Blossom. He's showed me places where big rocks were cast up on the mountainside after a cloudburst. But that was a long time ago. Look—the rain's stopping."

The sun came out as the clouds boiled away, driven by a sharp wind, and in a moment the mountains were diamond bright and already drying out in the sun. Angie and Jinx crawled out of the cave and looked up toward the shaft house. Bill Rolfe stood outside the door and he had the blue box open in his hands, putting something away in it.

He waved cheerfully when he saw them. Apparently he wasn't one to stay peeved long.

"Did you find any treasure?" Angie called up to him.

He shook his head. "Not the kind I'm looking for."

"How could he tell about treasure that quickly?" Jinx said. "I don't think he even has a flashlight along—unless there's one in that box."

She turned in her usual abrupt way and started back down the path and Angie followed her silently. There was a lot to think about now, a lot to wonder about and tell Mark.

By the time she reached the foot of the hill Angie found that her clothes were nearly dry—so quickly did moisture evaporate in Colorado. Blossom Creek tumbled along between its rocky banks as merrily as ever. Certainly it gave no sign of turning into a threatening wall of water.

11

Shadrach

Early the next morning there drifted over Blossom the aroma of coffee and bacon and eggs being cooked over a fire of pitch pine in a little potbellied stove. It didn't take long for Bill Rolfe to catch the appetizing scent and show up at the door of the Wetheral house.

Mom of course welcomed him in joyfully. There was nothing Mom liked better than to feed hungry men. That was one thing she could do a lot better than Clara, the efficient secretary in Dad's books. Clara couldn't cook at all.

Mom and Bill seemed to take to each other at once. If there was anything about this young man not quite to be trusted, Mom certainly did not sense it, Angie thought. And like the world in general, Bill adored Mom on sight.

"First time I ever spent a night in jail," he said, looking at them solemnly behind his horned rims.

"How was it?" Dad asked dryly. Dad never accepted people with the immediate and wholehearted liking Mom was so ready to give. He was sizing this young man up with his author's eye, as Angie could see. It was probably a good thing people didn't realize that he was apt to regard them as story possibilities and probe and analyze just for the sake of future fictional use.

Bill answered Dad's question carefully and in detail. There didn't seem to be very much humor in Bill Rolfe. He was tuned into life at a serious, scientific level. In answer to further questions from Dad, he admitted that he was a prospector of a sort—but he wouldn't tell them what sort.

"Just think of the enormous treasure storehouse that still exists mineral-wise throughout these mountains," he told Dad soberly. "Why, I'll bet man hasn't done more than scratch the surface!"

"He's been trying hard enough for the last hundred years," Dad said. "And it seems to me I've heard that a peck or two of gold and silver has been dug out of these mountains."

"Gold and silver!" Bill sounded scornful. "That's old stuff. In the gold-rush days they didn't have sense enough to think of the lead and zinc and copper and all the rest. They weren't even getting gold out very efficiently. Men came in years later and found there was still wealth to be got out of old mine dumps. And you mustn't forget the Curies."

"I wouldn't forget them for anything," Dad said. "What about 'em?"

Bill paused with a forkful of egg halfway to his mouth. "The first radium was found in a shipment of ore they got right in Gilpin County." The egg slithered off his fork and landed on the plate, spattering right and left, while Jasper Junior yelled with glee. Bill blushed and apologized and gave his complete attention to eating thereafter. A little later he went off—to have a "look at the field," he told them.

"An earnest young man," Dad said, when Bill had bumped his way out the door, first tripping over the sill. "And I expect he will eventually learn how to control his hands and feet."

"I like him a lot," Mom said brightly. "It's nice to find a young person who has a serious interest and a good appetite."

Dad went off chuckling to work at his typewriter. Guthridge Gilmore was definitely on the scene now and was giving his attention to identifying the battered body of a man who had been found at the bottom of an old mine shaft. "Beaten and then drowned," Dad explained cheerfully to anyone who was interested. "Because old mines are apt to fill up with many feet of water."

Fortunately such gruesome details never upset the rest of the Wetherals, or spoiled their appetites. It was accepted that this was a make-believe world that Dad lived in and you didn't get disturbed about it as you would over crime in real life. Besides, in Dad's books the criminals were always punished.

When Bill had gone, Mark announced that he had a date with Grandpa Kobler in his workshop and Angie pleaded to be allowed to go along.

"All right," Mom said. "But that means the two of you have to do lunch dishes. Now scoot—I can work faster with you out of the way. Jasper, no, no! That piece of bacon fell on the floor—give it to Mommy."

Jasper gave it to Mr. Gimmore instead, smearing the giraffe's face with a new layer of grease, while Angie shuddered and hurried out the door.

The morning was bright blue and gold, as seemed to be the rule for mornings in Colorado. White puffs of cloud might drift lazily into the sky in the afternoon, but most mornings were clear and cloudless. The pines on the mountain slope across the valley stood utterly motionless like pines in a stage-set. You wouldn't think they could moan and thrash their branches about as Angie had seen them do.

The two Wetherals went down the road toward the house with the cupola. Grandmother Kobler was out in the postage stamp of a front yard, working over a flower bed. She looked up, trowel in hand, as if she expected them.

"He's out in the work shack," she said sourly, as if Grandpa's talents irritated her. "He ought to be up on a ladder fixing those loose shingles on the roof. But you can't pry him away from those wood chunks once he gets started."

Following the direction in which Mrs. Kobler pointed with her trowel, Angie and Mark found the small log building down on the stream bank. Grandpa, looking out a window, saw them coming and waved them in, smiling a welcome. He seemed extra happy and cheerful, and Angie suspected that it was because he was doing this work with his hands that he enjoyed so much.

Before she went through the door, Angie glanced back at the house, hoping for a glimpse of Jinx, but the other girl was nowhere in sight.

"Come in, Angela, come in," Grandpa Kobler invited. Mark was already in, looking about him spellbound. This sort of room was obviously heaven to Mark.

"Built every bit of it myself," Grandpa Kobler told them. "Hauled the logs and chinked 'em and put on the roof. Of course I was a younger man in those days. How do you like it, boy?"

Mark's sigh of delight spoke for him. It was a nice enough workshop, Angie thought. Everything was shipshape and there were shelves along the walls, not only to hold tools and materials, but also to display some of the lovely wood figures Grandpa Kobler had made. But still Angie couldn't feel the surge of speechless delight that evidently filled her brother.

"It's very nice," she said politely.

That brought Mark to life. "Nice!" he snorted. "This is the most wonderful place I ever saw in my whole life!"

Grandpa Kobler beamed his pleasure. "I can see that you are a man after my own heart. Well, how about having a look in that wood box over there?"

Mark and Angie walked over to the indicated box, not quite sure what he intended. It was a large wooden box, of the type that held canned goods, and it was piled far above the brim with chunks, limbs, knots, and boles of wood.

"When Juanita and I bring in wood for burning in the fireplace," Grandpa Kobler said, "we pull out every piece that has possibilities and keep it here for me to work with. If you two want to try your hands at making some sort of critter or thing out of wood, you can find a piece that suits you and I'll show you how to start. But first you have to *see* something in the wood.

These things I make aren't carvings you know. The shape is already there and I just chisel it down and sand it till it looks like something."

Mark dived into the pile at once, knocking some of it to the floor in his haste. But Angie stood by doubtfully. Somehow this wasn't the sort of occupation that appealed to her, though she didn't want to be impolite to Grandpa Kobler.

"There's an elephant," Mark said, holding up a chunk of wood that bore no resemblance to anything as far as Angie could see. "This one looks like a boat. And golly, here's a baby chick!"

It all looked like fuel for a stove to Angie, and Grandpa Kobler quickly sensed her lukewarm interest. "If you don't hanker for this kind of tinkering yourself, Angela, maybe you'd just like to look around at the things I've already made."

That suited Angie better. So while Mark decided on the piece that he claimed looked like a baby chick, she wandered about the room, admiring the results of Grandpa Kobler's craftsmanship, while he gave her a running account of each object she touched. That bird with the pointed beak was made of aspen, while that comic-looking rabbit had been found in a pine burl. It was the pitch in the chunks of weathered pine that brought out the colors, he explained. Though of course you had to take off the surface and find your way down to the beautiful grain of the wood. That candlestick she was holding was made of limber pine.

"You've seen those twisted trees high up on the mountains where the timber line ends, haven't you? Well, that's limber pine. Feel how light it is compared to the rest. You can tell it by its gray-white color too."

Mark carried his cedar chunk over to Grandpa Kobler's workbench and the old man showed him how to go to work with a wood chisel and rasp, bringing out the shape of the chick that was so far only suggested in the wood.

Angie paused to look out one wide window of the workshop. The stream was almost directly below the building and it was always fascinating to watch the creamy rush of water as it broke over shiny wet rocks. Then she moved on to the next shelf and cried out in pleasure. Here, tiny and more delicate than anything else she had seen, were six little ballet dancers. Their arms were raised in different poses, their legs seemed to move in the steps of a dance.

"These are wonderful!" Angie cried. "How did you ever make them?"

Grandpa put down the wood he was sandpapering and came over to pick up one of the tiny figures. "So you like my little dancers, do you? Pick out the one you like best and you can have it for keeps."

"Oh, thank you!" Angie cried. She waved the little dancer of her choice at Mark, but he was deeply absorbed in chipping away with his chisel and she doubted if he even heard her. "But what are they made of?" she asked. "How did you make them?"

"Out of roots," Grandpa Kobler said. "Storm came along and washed away a lot of earth and these roots stuck up out of the ground. Bits of roots from old Shadrach, that's what they are."

Angie turned the figure slowly about in her fingers. "Did you say 'Shadrach'?" she asked with a catch in her breath.

Grandpa Kobler looked a little puzzled at her tone. "Why, sure. That's the name we gave him a long time ago—Ben Ellington and me."

Angie took a deep breath. "If there's a Shadrach, then there must be a Meshach—and—and Abednego."

"Guess that's right. At least there used to be. Just what are you getting at, Angela?"

Excitement bubbled over in Angie so that she could hardly make her words clear. "Oh, don't you remember? We asked you the other day in the cemetery if you knew something named Abednego, and you said you couldn't remember."

"That's right." The old man nodded. "Those two've been gone so long that I'd plumb forgot 'em. Now if you'd said *Shadrach* . . ."

"But where are they?" Angie demanded. "If Shadrach's still there—whatever it is—then maybe we can find where the other two were."

"Reckon we could," the old man said. "Tell you what, Angela, after a while when Mark gets tired of his job here, maybe we'll take a little walk and investigate."

"Oh, now!" Angie wailed. "We can't wait. Let's go now—right away. Mark, leave your old chicken for later. Come along!"

Like a swimmer coming to the surface, Mark popped out of his deep concentration and looked at her. "I'm not quitting now. Let it wait."

"But, Mark, it's the *treasure*. We've found Abednego!"

"That's fine," Mark said absently, more interested at the moment in the treasure he held in his hands. "If it's the treasure, it won't run away. First I'm going to finish this."

"Oh, you!" cried Angie and turned pleadingly to Grandpa Kobler. "Then can't you tell *me* where it is? I can go look by myself."

"Well now," there was a twinkle in Grandpa Kobler's eyes, "do you think that would be fair to your brother, Angela? Don't you think you can restrain your impatience just a mite longer till he gets as far as the sandpapering stage on that chick?"

She didn't want to wait. She regarded the other two with impatience, but at the same time realized that she was faced by the combined opposition of two men who had projects of their own in view. And she knew from sad experience what that meant. However, she felt that she couldn't wander around this workroom idly, waiting for them to get through. Neither could she rush wildly off and start digging unless Grandpa Kobler gave her some clue.

She left the workroom, taking the little root dancer with her and went to look for Jinx Kobler. This time she looked up at the tower window and saw Jinx sitting there watching her calmly.

"Hello," Angie called.

Jinx returned her greeting grudgingly, but made no move to leave her window and come down. Angie had hoped that their moment of friendship on the mountainside yesterday, when Jinx had spoken of her father and mother, might grow into a pleasant relationship.

"Do you want to come down?" she invited.

Jinx shook her head and stared off in the direction of the distant snowcaps.

"All right," said Angie determinedly, "then is it all right if I come up? I want to show you something your grandpa gave me."

"I can see it from here," Jinx said. "Giving you that spoils his set of dancers."

Grandmother Kobler, kneeling before the flower bed, had paid no attention to them. But now she straightened on her knees and looked up at the window.

"You know what manners are," she told her granddaughter sharply. "So just you mind them."

Angie began to wish she hadn't spoken to Jinx at all. It was one thing to persist herself, but it was something else when grownups interfered. She knew how much she would resent it if someone told her in front of other people to mind her manners and do something she didn't want to do.

"Never mind, Jinx," she began awkwardly.

"You can come up," Jinx said.

There was nothing else to do, so Angie went into the house and up the dark stairway, feeling more uncomfortable than ever. Everything she tried with Jinx seemed to be wrong.

The door at the end of the hall stood open and she hesitated on the threshold. Jinx still sat by the window, but she heard Angie's step and spoke to her tensely without turning. Her tone was low, so her grandmother couldn't hear.

"I'll be glad when you get out of Blossom. All of you. Then it will be the way it was before."

Angie went into the room and suddenly, as if she remembered something, Jinx turned and picked up a framed picture on her dresser and laid it face down in a single gesture. Angie sought for some answer to Jinx's words.

"What are you going to do when you grow up?" she asked. "You can't hide here in Blossom all your life. Besides, isn't your grandfather getting too old for this kind of life?"

"Grandpa's all right!" Jinx made an angry movement of rejection with her hand, caught the corner of the picture, and sent it flying across the room. It fell upon the rag rug at Angie's feet and there was the crunch of breaking glass.

Angie picked it up and turned it over. A long crack had splintered the glass and slivers fell out on the rug. It was an enlarged snapshot of a man and a woman. The man was tall and bore a clear resemblance to Grandpa Kobler. The woman was small and very pretty, with dark hair drawn down in smooth sections from a white part. Jinx snatched the frame from Angie's hands and looked at the broken glass as if she were going to cry.

"A new glass will fix it up all right," Angie said. "The picture isn't hurt."

"It wouldn't have happened if it hadn't been for you!" There was an alarming choke in Jinx's voice.

"I'll get it fixed for you," Angie offered hurriedly. "The next time Dad—"

"You will not!" Jinx hugged the picture to her and now tears were running down her cheeks.

Angie moved from one foot to the other and wished to goodness she had never come up here at all. But now that she was here she had to make some effort to soothe Jinx and mend the damage.

"Your mother was very pretty," she said softly. "You look an awful lot like her."

Jinx blew her nose and stared at Angie. "You don't need to say things that aren't true. Grandpa says my mother was beautiful."

"That's easy to see," Angie agreed. "And you *do* look like her. Anybody can tell that."

Above the dresser a tilted frame held a somewhat wavery mirror and Jinx looked into it wonderingly. Angie stepped up behind her.

"If you'd just loosen your hair out of those braids and not pull it back so tightly . . . if you brought it down over your ears the way she has hers . . . and of course you'd have to smile more. She looks like such a happy person."

Jinx studied the picture, her cheeks still streaked with tears. "Grandpa says she was always singing. She used to sing Spanish songs and Mexican songs. I wonder if she was happy."

"She had you and your father," Angie said. "Why shouldn't she be?"

Jinx put the picture face down on the dresser again. "A lot of good that did her. A lot that matters now."

"But you matter," Angie said, trying to figure it out herself. "You're part of them going on." Then, because Jinx looked as if she might get angry again, Angie tried the same trick that Mom used so often with Jasper— the trick of distraction. "You know what? I think we've located the treasure."

The trick worked. Jinx's attention was caught.

"What do you mean?" she demanded.

Angie explained about Shadrach and the roots from which the little dancers had been made. "So they must all have been trees," she concluded. "Shadrach, Meshach, and Abednego. And pretty soon your grandfather is going to show us where they stood. Maybe we can get him to come now."

She turned toward the door, hoping that Jinx would respond to the implied invitation in her use of "we." At any rate Jinx followed her down the stairs and they went out to the workshop together. Apparently Jinx meant to be in on any treasure hunt.

Mark's chick really looked like one now. The beak and pert little head and tail could be clearly seen and Mark viewed his handiwork proudly.

"I'm just about to the polishing stage," he announced. "So if we're going to dig for buried treasure, let's get started."

Grandpa Kobler put his tools away and made Mark clean up his chips and shavings before they went out. When everything was tidy, he led the way out the door, waving to his wife to let her know he'd be back before long. The direction he took was along Blossom's main street and he walked purposefully, as if he knew exactly where he was going.

At the Wetheral house he turned into the yard and gestured grandly. "There you are, Angela—there's old Shadrach, just the way he's stood for a whole heap of years."

Angie stared in amazement at the huge blue spruce in their very own yard, and Mark whistled his surprise.

"So *that's* Shadrach?" he said. "Then where did Meshach and Abednego stand?"

"You'll like as not find a couple of old stumps in the brush and weeds over on the other side of the yard. But don't ask me to tell you which was which. A blight hit 'em a long time ago and they both died. Only old Shadrach escaped. But I'm mixed up in my mind about which stood where."

He turned around and started toward the gate, and Angie called after him at once. "Aren't you going to stay and help us find the treasure?"

"Guess not," he said, smiling at her mildly. "I've seen about all the treasure I can take in one lifetime. Most of it belonged to other people and I never much liked what it did to them. Anyway treasure is for young folks like you. Good luck and you can let me know how you fare."

He went off down the road without a backward glance.

"He doesn't believe in it," Jinx said. "He doesn't think there is any treasure."

Angie and Mark paid no attention. They stood for a moment staring across the yard toward the place where brush and vines had grown up in a thick, concealing mat. Then they crossed the yard and began scrabbling among the weeds.

12

At the Foot of Abednego

Angie found the first stump by kicking it so hard that she hurt her toe and had to hop around for a minute before the stinging stopped. Mark discovered the second one a few feet away, chopped off close to the ground so you'd never have known it was under all the creepers if you hadn't been looking for it. Jinx had not joined in the search, but watched them solemnly from across the yard.

"So now," Mark said, "the digging begins. Do you want to help us, Jinx?"

Jinx shook her head. "Why should I? You won't find anything."

They ignored her and went into the house to look for a shovel and pick. The typewriter was silent, the house empty. In the middle of the grid on the now cold stove was a sheet of paper with chicken tracks across it—one of Mom's messages.

"They're out," Angie cried joyfully. "Now we can dig without being asked a lot of questions, or being laughed at if we don't find anything."

The message read: "Hv gn dn mt rd. Dd wnts Mr. G 2 hv lk @ lwr vly."

Jinx had followed them into the house and they all figured out the message together. Translated, it read: "Have gone down mountain road. Dad wants Mr. Gilmore to have look at lower valley."

Mark lost no time in picking up the shovel, while Angie armed herself with a broken bread knife they'd found in the yard, a garden trowel, and a poker. None of the latter looked too promising as tools for digging buried treasure, but they were all that came ready to hand.

It was Jinx who thought of the next problem before they left the kitchen. "Where're you going to dig first?"

They thought about that for a moment. "I guess it doesn't make much difference," Mark said. "One way we're wrong, one way we're right. There isn't any way to tell which to try first."

"So," said Jinx, "where are you going to dig?"

Mark, gazing thoughtfully around the room, as if to find some guidance in the arrangement of the furniture, uttered a sudden exclamation and pointed. Angie saw that for once Jasper had left Mr. Gimmore behind.

"Of course!" Angie cried, knowing what Mark meant. "Mr. Gimmore knows!"

Mark nodded. "Let's give the mangy old thing a chance to prove he's as smart as Jasper says he is."

Jinx stared as if they'd both gone crazy. "How can that silly giraffe tell you where the treasure is buried?"

"Oh, lots of ways," Angie said airily. "How will we work it, Mark?"

Mark picked up the giraffe which grinned at him greasily. "Come along. I'll show you."

When they reached the yard, he walked over to Shadrach and stood facing the big tree, his back to the two hidden stumps.

"Look," he said. "I'll just toss him straight over my head and whichever direction he falls in, we'll dig at the stump that's nearest."

"No," Angie cried. "Let me. After all, Waldo used to be mine before he turned into Mr. Gimmore. He knows me best."

Mark gave the toy up to her with a grin and stood back to watch. Jinx watched too in bewilderment.

First Angie whispered in the giraffe's one ear. This was terribly important, she told him, and he must do his very best to help them. Then she said, "One, two, three, away!" and tossed Mr. Gimmore high over her head.

He went straight up into the air and hooked himself into one of old Shadrach's branches.

"That's just fine," Mark said scornfully. "He's a smart one—Mr. Gimmore. And so are you. Now who's going to get him down?"

Jinx offered unexpected assistance. She kicked off her loafers, stuffed her socks into them, and scrambled up into Shadrach's lower branches like the little mountain "critter" her grandfather had called her. Angie held her breath lest she fall, but Jinx was obviously an old hand at climbing trees and in no time at all she had rescued Mr. Gimmore and dropped him down to them. Without giving Angie another chance, Mark caught him, whirled him three times around his head and tossed him backward.

This time he cleared Shadrach's branches and sailed across the yard, neck outstretched, and ear cocked. Without hesitation, as if he knew exactly where he was going, he tumbled head over heels toward the stump that was farthest from the road. Angie and Mark hurried over to attack the ground in front of it with great energy and little success. There seemed to be rocks everywhere, and the vines got in the way, as well as a bush with scraggly roots.

"I should think," Jinx said in a superior voice as she watched these futile operations, "that anybody who was going to hide a treasure would hide it behind the tree, not out in the front of the yard."

"O.K.," Angie said to Mark, "you dig where you are and I'll poke around behind."

She hammered the poker deep into the ground until it stuck. Then she made a face. "Another rock. How can we dig in ground that's mostly boulders?"

"Maybe you've hit the treasure," Jinx suggested. "If it's in a box it will feel like a rock."

"Let me try," Mark said and began to dig with his shovel beside Angie's poker.

It was the ring of the shovel on metal that told them Mr. Gimmore had known what he was doing. Even Jinx crossed the yard to watch more closely as Mark and Angie frantically shoveled and scooped the earth aside to reveal some sort of metal box buried not too deeply behind the stump that had once been a blue spruce named Abednego.

Mark knelt on the edge of the hole and bent to lift out the box. "Say! It's heavy. Or maybe it's just stuck."

In her excitement, Angie nearly slid into the hole herself. She tugged and pulled and, together with Mark, managed to free the box from its earthy prison and bring it up to level ground. Mark was right—it was heavy. There must be something of real value inside.

"It's probably full of rocks," Jinx said skeptically.

Angie brought out a broom and swept the loose earth from the surface of the box so that they could have a better look at their find. It was fairly large, irregular in shape, and not what one would expect of a strongbox in which treasure was buried. Once it had been painted a bright blue, though now only traces of the paint remained.

"That's the same color of blue as the door of the locked room," Mark said doubtfully.

"You know what it is?" Jinx said. "It's a breadbox. Just an old breadbox. And who'd bury treasure in a breadbox?"

"Maybe Uncle Ben would," Angie protested. "It must have been his box if it's the same blue paint he used on that door. Open it up, Mark."

Mark gave her a disgusted look. "How can I? Don't you see there's a padlock?"

For the first time Angie quieted down enough to see that the metal rings on the front of the box had been fastened together with a small padlock.

"Maybe one of the keys Mr. Bingham gave Mom will fit," Angie said. "They're hanging in the kitchen. Let's try."

She and Mark each took an end of the bulky box and carried it into the kitchen. Jinx waited for no invitation, but followed right along. In spite of the way she kept trying to discourage them, she apparently meant to miss nothing of what happened.

Angie tried one key after another, her fingers shaking with excitement, but not one of them was the right one. She and Mark looked at each other in despair. To get this close to the treasure and not be able to find out what it was was discouraging.

"If we had a file," Mark said, "I suppose we could file off the lock. But that would take a long time."

The three of them stood looking at the battered, once-blue box in the middle of the kitchen floor. Then Jinx leaned over and gave the top of it a resounding thump. It responded with a tinny ring.

"It's only tin," she said. "You can open it with a can opener."

Somehow it seemed all wrong to open a treasure box with a can opener, but Mark lost no time in getting one from the drawer of the kitchen table.

"O.K.," he said, "here goes!" and jabbed it into the top of the box. The sheet of tin was not too thick and he worked the instrument laboriously around the lid, cutting a sharp-edged hole. When three sides had been cut, he wasted no further effort, but bent the loosened piece up, revealing a newspaper-stuffed interior.

Angie tugged at the well-packed wad of paper that made up the top layer, pulled it loose, and tossed it to the floor. Then they all stood looking at what lay beneath. At first there appeared to be only more wads of newspaper stuffing the whole box. Jinx kicked the big piece on the floor out of the way through the living room door and came back to watch. Mark reached in to lift out one little package of paper.

"There's something in it," he told Angie. "Something heavy."

"Well, open it!" Angie cried. "Don't stand there looking at it!"

But Mark was not the son of a mystery story writer for nothing. This, his manner seemed to indicate, was where you built up the suspense. And not even his own interest in discovering what was wrapped in the paper was going to make him unaware of the attention of the two girls who made his audience.

He set the packet on the table with a dull thud. Then slowly, carefully, he poked up one folded-over corner, then another, until the paper seemed to crackle open of its own will, to reveal its long-buried secret.

There in the center of the torn scrap of paper was a chunk of black rock. Angie stared at it, limp with disappointment. Then, without waiting for further drama from her brother, she snatched at one newspaper parcel after another, unwrapped them in furious haste, tossing the paper on the floor as the contents of each came to light. When she was through, the box was empty and a pile of black rocks lay upon the kitchen table.

"Coal!" Angie wailed. "Just some old chunks of coal."

Jinx reached past her to pick up one of the rocks. "Don't be silly," she said. "That's not even coal. Coal's blacker than this and it's shiny, not dull." She began to laugh. "Treasure! Just some old hunks of black rock. Uncle Ben always liked to play jokes. And he sure has played a big one on you."

It took quite a lot to make Angie mad, but now excitement, disappointment, and irritation with Jinx all added up to a sudden outburst.

"You shut up!" she told Jinx furiously. "You shut up and go along home. We never invited you in the first place. You're mean and unkind. You'll never be anybody's friend. You go on home!"

Jinx stared at her with the astonishment she might have displayed if one of the chairs had suddenly bitten her. Then she flushed a dark, painful red, whirled about, and stalked through the living room and out of the house.

"Wow!" Mark said admiringly. "You sure told her off."

But Angie's fury died as swiftly as it had risen, and for a second she was tempted to run after Jinx and tell her she didn't mean a word of what she'd said. Now she'd made everything worse. But she knew that Jinx at this moment would certainly not listen to an apology.

"It's my red hair," Angie told Mark miserably. "Oh, why do I have to pop off like that every so often?"

"Don't blame your hair," Mark said. "Mom says red-haired people aren't any more quick-tempered than anybody else. It's just that old legend about red hair that encourages them." Then he turned back to the pile of rock on the table. "Well, I guess this is the end of our treasure hunt."

Angie made herself forget about Jinx. She put out a finger and counted the stones over twice. "There're seven of them, Mark. *Seven.*"

"So what?" Mark said.

"Don't you remember the map? Seven black diamonds. And here they are—our seven black diamonds. So don't you think they could mean something?"

"What?" Mark demanded, sounding discouraged. "It's just a joke, like Jinx says. Well, let's get this mess dumped out where it won't clutter up the kitchen and make Mom and Dad laugh at us."

He brought over a barrel Mom had been using for a trash basket and made a motion to sweep the stones into it. But Angie reached out to stop him.

"Wait a minute! Mark, there's just got to be an answer somewhere. He said we'd have to work for it with our heads and our hands—remember? I wonder if the paper the stones were wrapped in would tell us anything."

She picked up a scrap of paper from the floor and spread it open on the table, smoothing out the wrinkles. It was only a section from a "Help Wanted" column. Then she turned it over and gasped. Down the reverse side ran four blue pencil marks, underlining words. She picked the words out with her finger, reading them aloud, one by one.

" 'Substances,' 'she,' 'victim,' 'received.' "

"It doesn't make any sense," Mark said. But he picked up another scrap of paper and spread it on the table beside the first. Sure enough, this one too bore underlinings in blue.

Excitement began to rise in Angie again. She ran into her father's makeshift study, found a pencil and a sheet of yellow paper. Then she and Mark went to work hunting for every underlined word on the seven scraps of paper, while Angie listed them on the yellow sheet. Here and there a single number had been underlined and Angie put down the numbers too. When their search was completed, they had a list of fifteen words and numbers. Together she and Mark pored over it, trying to fathom the meaning.

THE LIST

substances	waste	8
she	killed	received
victim	honored	physics
discovery	they	1
8	9	wagon

Some of the words tantalized and hinted at a story. Someone had been a "victim," someone had been "killed," and someone had been "honored." Probably Dad could write a whole book around those words if he tried. But what they had to do with the seven irregular black rocks on the kitchen table, Mark and Angie hadn't the faintest idea.

"H'm," Mark said. "It sounds as if somebody had been doing some research in physics and had discovered some substances. But what do those numbers mean? And what has a wagon to do with it? And who was killed and why?"

"There just isn't enough to go on," Angie said. "If only there was more paper!"

Mark stared at her. "There *is* more paper. Don't you remember that very first wad you pulled out of the box? Where is it?"

Vaguely Angie recalled a motion on Jinx's part. Jinx had kicked the biggest wad of paper out of her way into the living room. In a second Angie was through the door, looking around. But nowhere in the living room was there a wad of old newspaper.

"Maybe she threw it outside," Angie said.

They bumped into each other trying to get through the narrow doorway at the same time. But no newspaper littered the yard.

"I'll bet she took it," Mark said. "Let's go after her."

They ran down the road to the house with the cupola, to find Jinx sitting calmly on the front steps, with Gold Strike asleep in her lap. Her face was no longer red, but she stared at them with dislike and suspicion.

Angie poked Mark into action. She just couldn't talk to Jinx right now herself.

"Hello," Mark said, trying his best smile. "Did you happen to pick up the old wad of paper that was stuffed in on top of those rocks?"

Jinx watched him defiantly. She looked a little like one of those mountain chipmunks that ran if you got too close to it and might bite if you touched it.

"Well," Mark said, losing his patience, "did you take it?"

"So what if I did?" said Jinx.

Mark moved to the bottom step. "Would you mind letting us have a look at it?"

"Why? What do you want with a piece of old newspaper?"

"Oh, nothing," Mark said calmly. "We just thought it might have some interesting stories or something."

"You're not fooling me," Jinx said. "I've got it, and I'm not going to give it to you. Not after the way *she* talked to me." She glared at Angie.

But Mark didn't take that sort of answer from a girl. He started up the steps and Angie wasn't sure what he might have done if Jinx hadn't been too quick for him. She sent the startled skunk flying out of her lap, jumped up, snatching the newspaper from under her in the same instant. Then she tore into the house and through to the kitchen.

Angie and Mark were on her heels, but Jinx moved

with the speed of a wild thing. She pried the lid off the small wood-burning stove that supplemented bottled gas, thrust the paper down upon the glowing coals, and then clattered the lid back on top. Mark grabbed the holder and snatched the lid off a moment later, but he was already too late. Angie watched their last hope of solving the mystery turn glowing red and crumble into black ash before their eyes.

13

Up in Smoke

Mark looked at Jinx in disgust. "What did you do that for? You know what you are—just plain poison."

"If you don't like poison, why don't you go away from here?" Jinx demanded.

Angie listened miserably. This time she felt no upsurge of anger. She could remember only that in the beginning she had wanted to make friends with Jinx and she had failed. She had done worse than fail. She had set Jinx against them. Now she felt sorry and uncomfortable and completely helpless.

"Why would you hate it so if we found the treasure?" she asked.

Jinx, who had been ready for sharp words, or a fight, was not prepared for Angie's gentle tone. In her surprise, she answered without hesitation.

"If there really is a treasure and it's found, then all sorts of people will come here. Blossom won't be ours any more. It will turn into a boom town and they'll build a good road through. I don't want those things to happen. There'd be worse than that too."

Mark looked gloomily down at the red coals, where scarcely a thread of white ash remained and banged the lid back on the stove.

"What do you mean—worse than that?" Angie asked Jinx.

"I should think you'd see. Unless there was treasure right on the ground Uncle Ben left you, it wouldn't belong to you anyway. It might belong to outsiders. It might even belong to my grandfather."

"Then I should think you'd want to help find it," Angie said.

"And have him get rich and send me off to a school someplace where everybody'd look down their noses at me and sneer because they thought I wasn't as good as they were!"

Angie listened in surprise to this sudden outburst. "Why would anybody think you aren't as good as anybody else?"

Before Jinx could answer, the sound of music drifted to them from the side veranda. Someone was playing a guitar, and someone else had joined in on a banjo.

Mark forgot about the stove. "Who's that?"

"Grandpa," Jinx said grudgingly. "And that Bill Rolfe fellow. Grandpa has loaned him a banjo."

"I'll go see," Mark announced and went through the house and out to the veranda.

But Angie had little interest in the music. "Why did you say you aren't as good as other people?" she repeated.

"I didn't say I wasn't," Jinx snapped. "But I don't want people who think they're better looking down on me. I—I wouldn't take it. I'd run away!"

"But why should anybody think he was better than you?"

Jinx took hold of the back of a kitchen chair with brown, tense hands. "Because I'm half Mexican, and Grandmother says most everybody looks down on Mexicans."

Angie stared at her. "That's the silliest thing I've ever heard in my life. My goodness, we Wetherals lived in Mexico one summer while Dad was writing a book about it, and we loved the Mexican people we met. There's one girl down in Taxco that I still write to." Angie felt more indignant by the moment as her words tumbled out. This was something twisted and wrong that had to be mended at once. She started resolutely for the kitchen door.

"Where are you going?" Jinx asked in sudden alarm.

Angie paused in the doorway. "To talk to your grandmother. I'm going to tell her about Mexicans!"

Jinx was at her side in a moment, a hand on her arm. This was a new Jinx—pleading, almost frightened. "Don't do that! Please don't try. It wouldn't do any good."

From the doorway where she stood Angie could see Mrs. Kobler out in the back yard bending over a galvanized wash tub, scrubbing on a board. She looked thin and work-worn and tired. But she looked also like the sort of person who would never in all this world change her mind once she had made it up. She must have been an awfully strict schoolteacher.

"You couldn't change her mind," Jinx said. "And it would only remind her. I mean, sometimes when I try to do what she wants and don't get too many things wrong, she forgets about my mother. But if you talked to her, she'd remember and everything would be bad again."

"What about your grandfather?" Angie asked. "He must have told you different. I know he wouldn't believe anything so silly. He liked your mother."

"Other people aren't like Grandpa," Jinx said shortly. "Don't you think I know? I've been down the mountain to school in the wintertime. The kids don't like me. They call me names. And when they have parties they never invite me. Why should I want to go away from Blossom? I like it here."

Angie was beginning to realize that here was a problem so big that only her mother would be capable of handling it. She herself had no idea of what to say to Jinx.

Out on the side veranda they were playing "Oh! Susanna!" and Angie could hear Mark whistling right along with the instruments. The fire had gone out of Jinx. Without another word she turned and went toward the front hall. Angie heard her going up the carpetless stairway and a few minutes later her door closed softly upstairs. At least she hadn't banged it.

Embarrassed at being left alone in someone else's house—particularly when she hadn't been invited in—Angie tiptoed down the hall and went out the front door. Around on the veranda guitar and banjo burst into a somewhat noisy rendition of "Camptown Races." Angie looked back from the road and Mark waved to her. "Hey, wait a minute, and I'll go with you."

She stopped, and Bill Rolfe put down the banjo he had borrowed from Grandpa Kobler and grinned at her. "You're invited to a concert tonight. Gramps and I are going to polish up our repertoire and put on a performance."

Grandpa Kobler stilled the strings of his guitar. "You're going to do the polishing up, young fellow. You've been hitting some pretty sour notes there."

"And Bill's going to teach me to play a ukulele," Mark announced, leaving the veranda to join his sister.

"Don't forget," Bill Rolfe called after them. "Invite your parents. This will be the biggest thing in Blossom tonight!"

"Where's this performance going to be held?" Angie asked as she and Mark started for home.

"Where else but the bandstand?" Mark said.

Angie couldn't help giggling. That little white bandstand with the tipsy slant was going to be surprised to be occupied by a "band" consisting of one guitar and one banjo. But anyway it sounded like fun.

"Look," Mark said, "the station wagon's back."

A sudden memory struck them both at the same time. A memory of black rocks piled on a kitchen table, and scraps of old newspaper littering the floor.

"Mom'll pin our ears back!" Mark cried.

They broke into a run and slammed through the front door.

"I hear the Mounties arriving," Mom said as they dashed into the kitchen. "If you two will kindly leave your horses outside, perhaps you'll be able to explain the meaning of all that rubbish strewn around the kitchen."

Angie looked around wildly. "Mom, what did you do with it? Our stones and all that paper?"

"The paper has gone into the stove." Mom held one last wad in her hands, but before she could reach the stove with that, Angie flew across and rescued it from the very lip of the stove.

"Oh, Mother! Our clues!" she wailed. "All our clues! And what did you do with our stones?"

"I'm the one to be fussing, not you," Mom said. "And now do hush—your father is trying to work. If you mean that dirty stone pile you left on my nice scrubbed table—I threw it out the back door, where it could keep the other rocks company. You're both too big to bring home half the outdoors the way you used to when you were little."

Neither Mark nor Angie attempted an answer. Mom didn't scold very often. But when she did there wasn't any use arguing with her. She sounded tired and a little cross, as if life in Blossom wasn't always easy for her.

Mark and Angie went out the back door, to find Jasper moping despondently in the little pocket of rock.

"Mr. Gimmore gone!" he protested the minute he saw them.

Angie and Mark looked at each other. They had completely forgotten poor Mr. Gimmore after he had served his purpose in the treasure hunt.

"Now don't you start bawling," Mark told his small brother. "Mr. Gimmore is a very smart giraffe and it's just like you always said—Mr. Gimmore knows. You'll find him out in the front yard if you go look. He's been doing some very hard work."

Jasper trotted off to search the front yard and the other two turned their attention to re-collecting their seven black stones. Mom had apparently scattered them right and left, because each one was in a different spot. But hunt though they might, one rock remained missing. Not that it mattered a great deal. Six meaningless lumps of stone were enough to be confused about anyway.

"But I wish we had more than this one scrap of paper." Angie sighed. "We might have missed something in the rest. At least it's a good thing I put the list of words we made in my pocket. I've still got that."

"Much good it'll do us after Jinx burned up the main sheet," Mark said gloomily.

The thought of Jinx made Angie turn thoughtful again. When Mark went back in the house, she sat down on a shelf of rock and put her chin in her hands.

Somehow the mystery of the treasure, and the problem of Jinx—a more hurtful problem than she had ever realized—were becoming more and more bound together in her thoughts. Finding the treasure—the real treasure, not just this pile of rocks—might help Jinx, whether she wanted to be helped or not. No matter what she thought, Jinx couldn't stay here in Blossom forever. She was just closing her eyes to the future when she thought that. Her grandparents were getting old, and she was growing up. She needed to get used to being out among people, and she had to get over the foolish idea that everyone was as prejudiced as her grandmother.

But all this was certainly a problem for Mom. The very first time she got her mother alone, without even Mark around, she would talk to her about Jinx. In the meantime she might as well have another look at that scrap of newspaper she had rescued from destruction.

She opened it and spread it against her knee. This time she would read every single word on the scrap— not just the ones that were underlined. But her careful study yielded nothing that shed any light on the mystery.

14

The Missing Stone

That evening, right after the supper dishes were done, the performers and the audience gathered across the road from the Wetheral house at the little bandstand. Mark and Angie and Mr. Wetheral carried over some chairs for the older members of the group, while the young ones sat on an army blanket spread on the ground. Everyone was there, and that included Mrs. Kobler, Gold Strike, and Mr. Gimmore.

Gold Strike, Jasper, and Mr. Gimmore were the only ones who didn't settle down to listen. This was the skunk's time for waking up, and he felt very energetic and curious. He circled the bandstand, his little black nose sniffing at every blade of grass, investigating every stray odor, searching out bugs and beetles. Young Jasper, with Mr. Gimmore clasped in his arms, was nearly as inquisitive and lively.

It was a lovely evening—just cool enough for sweaters, but not uncomfortable. Blossom Creek sang its own bubbly song and there was a sighing of wind through the pines in the canyon.

Grandpa Kobler and Bill Rolfe had set up camp stools in the least uncertain section of the bandstand floor, and Angie, sitting cross-legged beside Mark, watched as they picked the strings of their instruments, tuning up. Jinx had arrived later than anybody else and reluctantly occupied a far corner of the blanket. She was the only one who didn't seem to be enjoying herself. Even Grandmother Kobler, who had brought some

130

sewing along so as not to be idle, admitted to Mom that she liked to hear a good "sing" once in a while. Just so Grandpa didn't get the idea it could go on all day when there was other work to be done.

They started off with a tune that Angie had never heard before and that Bill had learned only that day. Grandpa called it the "Cousin Jack Song" and explained that it was one the Cornishmen used to sing. After they'd strummed through it a couple of times, he and Bill sang it together. Bill didn't always sing in tune, but he sure sang loud. The song had many stanzas, and since Bill didn't know them all, Grandpa sometimes sang alone.

It didn't take long for Bill to run out of the mountain tunes he'd just learned, so Grandpa sang a few more while his audience listened contentedly. An evening hush lay over the valley, and as shadows climbed the mountainside the yellow sunlight crawled away, leaving a purplish haze behind. Grandpa Kobler's voice was husky and soft and not very strong, but it somehow tugged at your heart and made you wonder about the days when he had been strong and young and handsome—like that picture of his son.

Angie stole a look at Jinx and saw that her sullenness had fallen away as she listened to the plaintive songs her grandfather strummed on his guitar. These were tunes to make you feel pleasantly sad, and Angie edged over on the blanket closer to Dad's chair. Somehow his hand was hanging over the arm, just as if it waited for her own to slip into it. His hand was big and warm and gave her the feeling that as long as she held onto it she was safe and nothing hurtful could ever touch her.

Then Grandpa switched into the strains of "Pony Boy" and the spell was broken. They sang the old and familiar after that, and pretty soon everyone was singing, including Jasper, who ran round and round the bandstand, sometimes chasing Gold Strike, sometimes being chased by him, all the time chanting lustily his own out-of-tune songs. The old ghosts of Blossom must be stirring in their dim, forgotten corners, Angie thought. Perhaps the Cornishmen who lay beneath aspen and pine in the old cemetery heard the music in the depths of their long sleep. Perhaps Uncle Ben heard it too and was glad that folks could still sing in Blossom town.

When there was a little pause and everyone laughed and rustled about, Grandpa Kobler asked for requests. Later Angie could never figure out how that particular song happened to pop into her mind. Perhaps if she had stopped to think she would never have dared suggest it. But now she called it out suddenly, in a voice everyone could hear:

"Let's sing 'Juanita.' "

Grandpa Kobler looked down at her for a moment. He wasn't smiling now, but there was a gentleness in his eyes. He strummed a few chords and began to sing in his whispery voice:

"Nita—Jua-a-a-nita . . ."

It was beautiful and tender. No one joined in the first time, but they sang the second chorus softly together and even Bill brought his tone down almost to a whisper. Angie didn't dare look at Jinx, but she was aware of her there on the far corner of the rug, tense and still and listening. When she looked at Grandmother Kobler, she saw that the old lady wasn't singing. She sat stiffly in her chair, the needle in her hand quiet, her mouth straight and grim.

Oh, dear, Angie thought. Now Grandmother Kobler had been reminded of those things she wanted to forget, and perhaps she would make it harder than ever for Jinx.

When the song was over, Mom leaned toward Jinx and smiled.

"That was for you, Juanita," she said, and Angie experienced a deep surge of warmth toward her mother. Mom might not know all the trouble Jinx was in, but she always had the right instinct toward people. She always knew how to do the right thing. Angie darted a quick look at the other girl and saw that Jinx's dark

eyes were misty with tears. She saw something else surprising too, that she hadn't noted before.

Jinx had loosened her hair out of pigtails so that it
was no longer pulled back skintight, but fell in smooth
dark wings over her ears, and was clasped with a bar-
rette to hang loose on the back of her neck. The result
took some of the peaked sharpness out of her face and
made her look surprisingly like the picture Angie had
seen in Jinx's room.

Grandpa Kobler strummed some chords again and
announced an intermission. They all got up and
stretched and Bill leaned on the somewhat rickety rail
of the bandstand to watch Jasper and Gold Strike. Jasper caught Bill's eyes upon him and promptly trotted
over to the bandstand steps and climbed them on all
fours. Angie, watching in amusement, saw Jasper hand
something to Bill.

Whatever it was, Bill accepted it gravely. "Just what
I needed," he said, and dropped it with a clatter on the
floor beside him.

As it fell Angie recognized what it was. So that was
what had happened to their missing black diamond.
Young Jasper had picked the stone up for his own treasure pile. Before Angie could move to get it back, the
little boy picked up the stone and presented it to Bill
again.

"Well, thanks, fella," Bill said. "I sure appreciate
this."

He tossed the stone in his hand a couple of times
and seemed to become suddenly aware that it was
heavy. He weighed it once or twice on his palm and
then looked at it closely. There was such a strange expression on his face that Angie watched him in fascina-
tion. He put his banjo down, got up without warning,
and hurried down the steps and off toward his jail at a
pace that sent up clouds of dust.

"What's eating him?" Mark said.

Angie shook her head. "I don't know. But he's got
our seventh stone."

Bill was gone only a few moments and no one else

seemed to miss him. Mom was talking to Mrs. Kobler. Dad peered with interest through the latticework around the bottom of the bandstand as if he was studying something, while Jinx walked down to watch the tumbling water in the creek. No one except Angie and Mark noticed when Bill came hurrying back down the road.

He went at once to the edge of the bandstand and held the rock up to Jasper. "This is a pretty nice present, fella. Want to tell me where you got it?"

"Present," Jasper repeated, smiling at him through the railing.

"That's right," Bill said. "A present. You gave it to me. Now just tell me where you found it in the first place."

"Jasper wanta present," Jasper said happily.

Bill knew defeat when he saw it. Young Jasper had a one-track mind and it wasn't going down the track Bill wanted it to. He turned away helplessly and discovered Angie and Mark watching him.

"Say, do you two kids know anything about where your baby brother found this hunk of rock?"

"Why do you want to know?" Mark asked cautiously.

Bill looked down at them from his six-foot height, his eyes earnest behind horn rims. "Oh, no special reason. You know me—just an old rock collector. This might be an interesting specimen."

"Of what?" said Mark.

The older boy and the younger one eyed each other and Angie knew that Bill was going to be just as cautious as Mark.

"I'll tell you," Bill said, "if you'll tell me."

"What do you want to know?" Mark asked.

"Where this piece of rock came from."

"We don't know," Angie said quickly before Mark could answer. That was perfectly true. The fact that they'd dug it out of the ground in an old breadbox would hardly be the answer Bill would want. Where the rock had come from originally they hadn't the slightest idea. But if it was something as important as Bill seemed to think, then there *was* a treasure and they'd better find it before Bill did.

"O.K.," Bill said. "If that's the game you want to play. It's just an old hunk of black rock—no good to anybody." But he dropped it into the patch pocket of his jacket and wouldn't give it back when Mark asked for it.

Then Grandpa Kobler called them together for a few more songs before it got dark, and Bill went back to the bandstand. Dusk was painting Blossom with its gray brush and already there were stars in the deep blue overhead. Stars that seemed very close here in the mountains.

When there was a pause in the singing, it was startling to hear the sound of a car coming from the canyon road. They all looked around in surprise to watch its headlights shine upon the bridge and then catch the hillside in a moving arc of light as it made the turn and swung down the road toward them. The headlights shone directly on the little group around the bandstand and the driver braked his car and pulled to a stop a few feet away.

"Is that you, Mr. Wetheral?" called a thin, reedy voice, and a moment later Mr. Bingham, Uncle Ben's lawyer from Boulder, got out of the car and walked stiffly toward them.

Dad went over to shake hands and Mr. Bingham grumbled right through the greeting. It seemed that he had started out from Boulder very early that morning and had expected to be well on the way home by now. But engine trouble had halted him for repairs and he was later than he had intended to be.

"I don't like to drive these mountain roads at night," he concluded testily. "Too many curves and dropping-off places."

Dad managed to break in long enough to introduce him to the Koblers—whom he appeared to know about—and to Bill Rolfe. Grandpa Kobler invited him to spend the night with them.

"Plenty of room in our big house," Grandpa said, "and we'll be glad to put you up."

"Thank you," said Mr. Bingham without warmth. "In that case I will avail myself of your hospitality at once. This has been a very difficult day. Mr. Wetheral— if you will give me a little time in the morning—"

"Of course," Dad said, and Mom quickly invited him to breakfast.

So that was the end of the concert. Bill picked up the banjo to carry it back to the Koblers' and the party began to break up. Jinx seemed to fade into thin air. When Angie looked around for her, the girl was gone—without having spoken a word to anybody all evening. Angie wished she could have told her that her hair looked nice the new way.

Suddenly, startling everyone, Dad snapped his fingers with a loud click. "I've got it! I've finally got it!"

"Yes, dear?" Mom said calmly.

"I'd have you know," Dad announced, "that Mr. Guthridge Gilmore has just discovered the second body. My stooges will kindly ask me where."

"Where?" cried Angie and Mark together.

Dad pointed dramatically. "Right over there under the bandstand."

With an extremely pained expression, Mr. Bingham set off toward the Koblers', walking at the side of Grandmother Kobler, who appeared as little amused as himself. Mr. Bingham, Angie felt, would never understand a writer of mystery stories. The bandstand was a really good place for hiding a body. Temporarily, of course.

The Wetherals parted Jasper and Gold Strike, who were having a tug of war over Mr. Gimmore. The little skunk went waddling off on evening investigations and the Wetherals went into their own house.

"You shouldn't have shocked Mr. Bingham like that," Mom told Dad as he lighted the lamps. "I'm sure he is having a difficult time getting used to us as it is."

"I wonder what the old boy is up here for," Dad

mused. "He didn't make that mountain drive for his health. He's got something on his mind."

Angie went to bed wondering what it was. Mr. Bingham was connected with Uncle Ben and the will and the treasure. But what she wondered about most was why Bill Rolfe had seemed so interested in that chunk of black rock.

15

A Plan for Action

Angie's second study of the scrap of paper she had rescued when Mom was burning up the rest had led to nothing new, but she and Mark were still puzzling over the list of underlined words they had collected.

The next morning before breakfast they studied the list again, this time trying to make something out of the numbers. Perhaps they referred to a year, Mark suggested and they wrote down the possible years they could get from the numbers 8-9-8-1.

1988
1898
1889

The first one didn't seem likely. So that left them the other two.

"It must be," Mark said, "that either in 1898 or in 1889 some important discovery was made in connection with physics, or substances, or something. By somebody who was doing research. A woman probably, since 'she' is used."

"Maybe a man and a woman," Angie said. "Since 'they' is given. If we were home, we could get to the library and look it up. But how are we to figure out by ourselves what happened in 1889 or 1898?"

"I'll ask Bill Rolfe," Mark said. "He knows a lot about science. I'll ask him right after breakfast."

Mr. Bingham drove up just then, and Mom went to

the door to welcome him. This being a special occasion, she'd set up the table in the living room, instead of in the kitchen, and breakfast was to be served in style.

Their guest seemed surprised to find what livable quarters the Wetherals had managed to fix up for themselves. He was finicky about breakfast and wouldn't eat eggs, but had a single strip of bacon, some coffee, and toast. Mom's coffee seemed to mellow him a little and he became more chatty and human.

His "chat" took the form of some odd questions that made no sense at all to the Wetherals. Had they, he wanted to know, found anything of really remarkable interest or value since they had come up here?

That question launched Dad on an enthusiastic report on the wonderful background material he was collecting for his book, right here in Blossom. Yes, indeed, he had found plenty of interest and value. But that wasn't what Mr. Bingham meant, and finally, after two or three more roundabout questions, he came to the point.

"You might as well know," he said, "that there is a second part to Mr. Benjamin Ellington's will. I have in the safe at my office an envelope which was to be opened some days after the will had been read. Following instructions, I opened it. There was a second sealed envelope. If certain conditions had been fulfilled, I was instructed to open the second envelope. If these requisites were not fulfilled by the end of this year, then the envelope was to be burned unopened and the matter was to be closed."

"My goodness!" Mom said. "This sounds like a Jasper Wetheral mystery. What are the conditions?"

Mr. Bingham took another swallow of coffee and handed her his cup for more. "I am most regretful, Mrs. Wetheral, but I am not at liberty to divulge the details until the requirements have been met."

Dad seemed to think the whole thing was nonsense and took the attitude that this, more than ever, proved that Uncle Ben had reached a childish state where he enjoyed playing games. Mom tried a little Irish blarney on Mr. Bingham, but while he seemed to enjoy it in his own stiff way, he was obviously not going to tell them any more.

After breakfast he told Dad to be sure to get in touch with him if anything unusual occurred and then prepared to leave. That was when Angie got an idea. While Mark went off to talk to Bill Rolfe, and while Dad and Mom stood at the door of the car bidding Mr. Bingham good-by, she went down the road a little way and waited for his car to come along. She waved as he approached and he drew impatiently to a stop on the road beside her.

"What is it, young lady?" he asked.

He wasn't a very friendly person to talk to, but Angie did her best.

"I just wanted to tell you that something unusual *has* happened," she said. "Something Dad and Mom don't know about."

"Most unwise," said Mr. Bingham. "Children should always confide in their parents. And what was this unusual occurrence?"

"The only reason we didn't tell them was because we thought they would probably laugh. But we found the Abednego mentioned on those treasure maps Uncle Ben gave out, and we found an old breadbox buried at the foot of it."

"A breadbox?" Mr. Bingham echoed.

Angie wriggled uncomfortably. "I know it sounds queer. But Uncle Ben must have put the rocks in it and buried it for some purpose."

"Rocks?" said Mr. Bingham.

Angie flushed and brought her hand out of her blue jeans pocket. In it was one of the black stones.

"He—he said we'd find some black diamonds and—and this is what was in the box."

Mr. Bingham wasted no second glance on the stone. He smiled at her thinly and nodded as if she had been the age of Jasper Junior.

"I can understand why you wouldn't tell your parents. This must have been some joke of Mr.

Ellington's. I wouldn't worry my head about it any further if I were you. Good day."

He put the car into gear and drove off, leaving her standing there in the dust raised by the wheels. If she had been Jasper's age she was sure that she would have made a face at the retreating car. Somehow she had hoped that Mr. Bingham would react to the stone as Bill Rolfe had and that he would give them some of the answers. Well—she'd made a try and there was nothing more to be done at the moment.

When she got back to the house, she found Jasper playing in the yard and Mom doing breakfast dishes, while Dad worked at his book again. Mark was with Bill, and this was her looked-for opportunity to talk to Mom about Jinx.

She picked up a dish towel and got busy while she explained. Mom listened gravely, sympathetically. And when Angie got to the part about Mrs. Kobler telling Jinx that she wasn't as good as other people because she was part Mexican, Mom forgot all about the dishes. She waved her sudsy hands in the air indignantly and agreed that Jinx must certainly be helped as soon as possible.

"Do you suppose," Mom said, "that Jinx could come and visit us in Boulder for a week or so when we go home?"

Angie thought about that and shook her head. "I don't think you could pull her out of Blossom the way she feels now. I think the idea of visiting anybody would scare her to pieces."

"I expect you're right," Mom went back to swishing the dishcloth over plates and cups. "We mustn't move too fast. The very first thing is to make friends with her."

"I've tried," Angie said. "But she won't be friends. She just says she'll be glad when we all leave Blossom."

Mom considered the matter while they finished the dishes. Then she looked at Angie, her red head tilted to one side, her blue eyes lively, the way they were when she was working out a plan for action.

"I know something we can try. Now you listen and do just what I say."

Angie listened and Mom ran through the idea twice. It sounded good and it also sounded like fun. Mark would be mad to be left out, but this would be just for Mom and the two girls.

"So you go over and talk to Jinx right now," Mom concluded. "And remember—make it sound as though she would be doing us a favor."

Angie hurried off to the Koblers' at once and was glad to find Jinx in her grandfather's workshop, watching the old man rub candle wax on a pine piece he was finishing, to give it polish and sheen. Jinx's hair was in tight braids again and Angie thought it best not to mention the change last night. There was never any telling what might make Jinx mad.

She explained about Mom wanting to go on a picnic up in the hills, and not knowing an interesting place where they might go. "She thought you'd know a place where you could take us. There'd be just the three of us—Mom and you and me. And we'd bring our lunches and hike and rest and eat and have fun. Mom doesn't always like to go with Dad and Mark because they travel too fast for her. But she thought you might be willing to take us on a sort of slow hike that wouldn't be too far away."

While Angie was talking, Jinx stared out the workshop window and there was no telling if the other girl had even heard. But after a minute Jinx spoke suddenly.

"I know a place," she said. "It's a high mountain meadow—maybe an hour's climb above the canyon that leads into town. It's a place I like."

"That's wonderful!" Angie said warmly. "I'll go right home and tell Mom you'll help us out. Let's make it tomorrow morning."

Jinx looked bewildered at the suddenness of what had happened, and Angie rushed off before she could change her mind.

Mark was waiting for her in the road in front of their house.

"Where've you been?" he demanded. "I've been looking all over for you." He wasn't really interested in where she had been, but hurried right into his own news. "I know what the year was, Angie. 1898. And I know what happened in that year."

He waited dramatically.

"Well, for goodness' sake go on!" Angie cried.

"That was the year the Curies discovered radium. They were making their experiments with waste ore from right here in Colorado. All those words on our list fit into the Curie story."

"What about 'wagon'?" Angie said. "What has a wagon to do with it?"

Mark looked especially pleased with himself. "That's the word that checks the whole thing. Some of the rest might apply to other experiments. But don't you see—someone was killed, someone died a victim. That was Pierre Curie. He was killed on the street by a wagon that ran him down. But in 1898 he and his wife discovered radium. Angie, it all checks."

"But what does it *mean?*"

Mark gave her a disgusted look. "It's a good thing *I* talked to Bill Rolfe. He didn't catch onto what I was after for a while. But he got interested when I told him I was trying to figure out something in history that happened in 1889 or 1898 and had to do with an important scientific discovery. He popped out with the Curies before he meant to. And he knew how Pierre Curie died too. He didn't get cautious until I began to ask him about radium. Gosh, Angie—don't you get it?"

Angie shook her head. She didn't get anything at all.

Mark had one of the black stones in his hand and he waved it at her. "Don't you know what this is?"

"Of course I don't know what it is!" Angie cried.

"It's what radium comes from. *Now* do you know?"

She could only stare at him blankly.

"Pitchblende," Mark said. "That's all it is—pitchblende."

Angie felt unaccountably disappointed. "Is radium so very valuable?"

"Sure it's valuable. But radium's old stuff. There's something else they get from carnotite and some other ores, *and* from pitchblende."

"Well, why don't you tell me what?" Angie wailed.

Mark's voice held a touch of awe in it. "Uranium," he said. "What all the world is looking for—uranium. Somewhere right around these hills there may be a valuable deposit of pitchblende. When Bill Rolfe saw that stone, he knew. That's the treasure he came up here prospecting for, and boy! it's real treasure."

16

Picnic
in the Mountains

That night at the dinner table Mark and Angie decided that the time had come to tell Dad and Mom about the breadbox, the underlined words, and finally about the fact that Bill Rolfe had identified the black stones as pitchblende. Now, as Mark pointed out, the matter was no longer something the grownups could laugh off.

Grownups, however, were unpredictable. Mom and Dad listened, it was true, but their reactions were not in the least sensible.

Mom said: "Oh, goodness! Let's not go discovering any more uranium. It just means more atom bombs and all that."

"It's used for other things too," Mark put in. "Good things."

But Mom remained unexcited. Dad's reaction might have been expected. He thought the whole idea was wonderful and just what he could use in his story.

"H'm, pitchblende," he said. "The modern touch. Just the thing for developing stronger motivation on the part of the murderer. This will give him a wonderful reason for killing. Wait until Mr. Guthridge Gilmore hears about this!"

"Oh, Dad!" Angie cried. "This is real. There *is* some pitchblende around here somewhere. And Uncle Ben must have known about it."

145

Dad came down to earth and smiled at her kindly. "Honey, don't you think you're old enough now to get this treasure-digging idea out of your head? After all, suppose this deposit—if there was one—was actually discovered, what could it possibly mean to you?"

"Not to Angie and me," Mark said. "To you, Dad. If we found the treasure, then maybe you could take time to write your novel."

"And maybe we could stay right here in Colorado while you wrote it," Angie said.

Dad reached around the table and put an arm about each of them and gave them a good tight hug. "So that's what you two have been worrying about! But you mustn't worry about my problems. Things will work out all right—you'll see."

Mom left her place and ran around to drop a kiss on Angie's nose and then tuck one back of Mark's ear, where it always tickled, while Jasper banged his spoon on his plate so that he'd get some attention too. Angie couldn't help feeling happy and comforted just to know that Dad and Mom appreciated what they had been thinking about. But she was still interested in the treasure.

"The trouble is," Dad said, being serious about their announcement for the first time, "that all this mountain land, except for Government preserves and parks, is owned by individuals. Even if you found this pitchblende, it would probably belong to someone else."

"Then why is Bill Rolfe working so hard looking for it?"

Dad shook his head. "I can't answer that one. The spirit of adventure perhaps."

Angie had been listening in silence, but now a thought struck her. "There's still that other envelope that Uncle Ben left with Mr. Bingham. What if he willed this deposit, or whatever you call it, to us?"

"I'm beginning to think anything is possible," Dad said.

But Mom shook her head. "Don't count on that, Angie. I'm sure if Uncle Ben was going to will it to anyone, it would be to the Koblers, who were his old friends."

"Then I'd still like to find it," Angie said stoutly. "Maybe Jinx needs it even more than we do."

After that the discussion went on to other things, one of them being their return in another week to Boulder. Which left very little time, Angie thought, to discover a deposit of pitchblende that had lain hidden all these years.

The next morning she had little time to worry about buried treasure, however. Sandwiches had to be made for the picnic, and since bread was not their most plentiful item, they opened some canned brown bread and made sandwiches with cheese spreads and peanut butter.

As soon as Mark heard about this feminine picnic, he put up a protest. Why couldn't he go too? It wasn't fair to have a picnic and leave him out. And so on for quite a while. Mom held quietly to her intention, explaining that this might be an opportunity to talk to Jinx—something that might be harder to do with a boy along. Eventually Mark announced that he wouldn't go on a sissy picnic anyway. He'd go prospecting with Bill Rolfe.

"I'm afraid you can't do that," Mom told him firmly. "Dad is going to spend the day working on his book and someone has to take care of Jasper."

Having to be a baby sitter disgusted Mark all the more, but he knew when Mom meant what she said. The next yowl came from Jasper Junior. Mr. Gimmore was gone again. Everyone was too busy or too cross to search for the giraffe, so nothing was done to solve that problem. Probably, as Angie pointed out, Gold Strike had taken him again. The little skunk seemed to have developed a special fondness for Jasper's Mr. Gimmore.

Then Jinx arrived, bringing some chocolate cake her grandmother had baked especially for their picnic. For once she looked cheerful and interested, and seemed eager to show Angie and her mother something of her beloved mountains.

The trail she led them along started up the steep side of the canyon that was the entrance to Blossom. The real road followed the opposite side of the canyon, with the creek rushing along between the two banks.

As they climbed, the red pinnacles of rock that rose in the canyon took on the weird shapes of turrets and castles and monsters. Here and there tiny pine trees grew in mere crevices of rock where you'd think there'd be no roothold. As they climbed still higher, they could see the occasional deep gulches that cut down the mountainside opening into the canyon. At one point they reached a rocky crag where they could look down upon the very place where gulch and canyon met.

The day was windy and clouds raced over the sky. Warm as she grew from climbing, Angie was glad to have her jacket along when they paused for a rest at the edge of a pine forest. When they started out again, the trail turned away from the canyon rim and cut deep into a forest of tall, cool pines.

Jinx was in her element now and seemed a different girl. Sometimes she left the path to clamber up a pile of rock where she could view the country. Angie would have followed her, but Mom said no, because she wasn't as sure-footed as Jinx. But when the spot wasn't dangerous, Angie took side routes too, though the effort left her puffing as they climbed higher.

Down in the tight little valley of Blossom most of the high peaks were hidden, but now, when they came out of the forest into a mountain meadow, the real grandeur of the Rockies rose about them. There were jagged peaks with snow in their saddles and nearby an ice-blue mountain lake.

"This is the place I picked," Jinx said, waving a hand toward the gently sloping hollow of flower-dotted meadow before them. "I could take you farther. I could take you where you could make snowballs of glacier snow—if you want to go."

Mom shook her head. "This is very nice and I think it's about far enough for me."

She would have sat right down on a nearby rock, but

Jinx beckoned them on. "Let's eat down there in the hollow. I want to show you something. I brought you here for something special."

There was no trail now. Grass grew high and pines crowded the edge of the meadow. Blue lupine grew everywhere and there were stalks of orange-red Indian paintbrush. Jinx, walking ahead, paused to kick at something half hidden by the grass.

Mom stumbled. Stooping to see what had caught her toe, she uttered an exclamation. "Angie, Jinx, look! Here's part of an old door."

Angie looked about and saw that here and there, buried in deep grass, lay old timbers, bits and pieces of buildings which had once stood in this mountain hollow.

"There used to be a town here," Angie said, her voice soft, as if she must not wake what lay sleeping.

"That's right," Jinx said. "This was the town of Farewell. A few years ago it was like Blossom. But there was nobody to look after it the way we look after Blossom. So the buildings tumbled down. People came and carried the timbers away to burn for fires. And now there are just the old bones left."

"Old bones," Mom echoed. "That's a good way to put it. We'll never see anything like this again. I'm glad you brought us here, Juanita."

Jinx glanced quickly at Mom, but offered no objection to her use of the name. Mom, as Angie could see, was making friends with Jinx in her own special way, as she herself had never been able to do.

They found some old steps that climbed into empty air and sat down on them to open their lunch boxes. The wind moaning in the pines made a lonesome sound and the high little meadow that had once been the town of Farewell seemed remote from all the rest of the world. Far above, the high peaks looked down on them sternly, their slopes thinly polka-dotted with pines as the timber line was reached.

"Do you know what we'd love, Juanita?" Mom said, biting into her second brown bread sandwich.

Jinx shook her head and waited.

"We'd love to have you come and visit us in Boulder after we go back there in another week."

Jinx was plainly startled, but for once she made no angry, impatient move. "Oh, I—I couldn't!" she said.

Mom, however, once she set after something, was never easily discouraged. "Of course you don't know us very well," she went on. "But don't you think you could like us enough to come visit us for a week or so?"

"I don't want to go away from Blossom," Jinx said tensely. "I wish I didn't ever have to go away from Blossom."

Gently Mom reached out and took one of Jinx's small brown hands in hers. Jinx looked uncomfortable, but she didn't pull away.

"Angie has told me how you feel about Blossom, and how you feel about the world outside. But you can't hide from that world for always, Juanita. Wouldn't it be easier to come out once in a while on a visit to friends?"

Jinx stuck out one toe and set a blue aspen daisy nodding. "They don't want me—out there. And I don't want them."

"We want you," Angie put in. It was funny really, how she had grown to like Jinx in spite of her prickly ways. Somehow she had the feeling that underneath the unfriendliness was someone who was all alone and needed help. Jinx was like a lost kitten that scratched at you because she was frightened.

"That's right," Mom agreed, "we do want you, Juan-ita. And we think that if you come out of that shell of yours proudly—because after all, you have a lot to be proud about—other people outside will like you as much as we do."

Jinx wriggled her fingers out of Mom's grasp and slumped down to the bottom step. "You're just making those things up. Nobody ever likes me. What have I got to be proud about?"

Mom popped her last crumb of sandwich into her

mouth, clasped her hands about her knees, and leaned
against the weathered steps. She studied Jinx calmly as
if she were seeing her for the first time.

"Well, now, let me see. . . . You're very pretty, for
one thing. Of course that's something to be grateful for
rather than proud of, since we don't pick our looks.
But all of us have to make the most of what we have.
When you smile you're pretty. When you look like a
thundercloud—well, you look like a thundercloud.
Some of the time you're a very smart girl. And you
know dozens of things we city people never have a
chance to find out."

Jinx stared. Plainly no one had ever talked to her
like this before. Then she scowled and shook her head.

"What good would it do me in the city to know
mountain things?"

"I think it does anybody good anywhere to have
some special sort of knowledge. Those city things
you're afraid of are easily learned. Probably mountain
things take a lifetime. Then there's your wonderful, ex-
citing background."

Jinx grew very still. "My what?"

"Being the daughter of a beautiful Mexican girl,
Juanita. Angie has told me about the picture in your
room."

"I only want to be an American," Jinx said.

"Of course we all want to be that. But just as I'm
part Irish and proud of it, and as your grandmother is
proud of her Cornish people, you have a heritage to be
proud of. All together we contribute to the whole rich
picture that makes up America. You have to remember
that the Mexicans are a wonderful people. They're gay
and full of music and spirit. They're generous beyond
anything we understand. And they're creative and artis-
tic."

"They're dirty and lazy," Jinx said, and Angie
gasped.

It took a lot to make Mom angry, just as it did with
Angie, but when she did get mad she did a really good,
spark-spitting job of it. She looked at Jinx now and

Angie could see that the sparks were getting ready to fly. Even the red curls at her mother's temples trembled with indignation. Jinx stared at her startled. It was easy to see that her words had set off a charge.

"I thought you were a really smart girl who was just making a few natural mistakes," Mom snapped. "But now I know that you're just prejudiced and unkind and foolish."

Jinx's lips parted in astonishment, but she could make no suitable answer.

Mom tried to restrain her wrath and speak more gently. "Probably there are Mexicans who are lazy and dirty. So are there lazy, dirty Americans and English and French and anybody else you can name. But you can only judge the one in front of you. Right now I see a girl in front of me who is a quarter Cornish, a quarter mixed American, and one half Mexican. Judging just the one in front of me, I can say that she goes out of her way to make people dislike her—even when they want to like her. That instead of standing up to the outside world with courage and showing it that she is someone to be respected for her own self, she wants to hide in the mountains and either run from people or fight them. But I'm not going to judge all Cornish-Mexican-Americans by this one rather silly little girl."

Jinx made one last effort. "But my grandmother says—"

Mom didn't let her finish. "Your grandmother grew up with her prejudiced ideas. No one ever taught her a better way and she can't help what she believes. But you have a mind of your own and you can think this out for yourself. It's pretty foolish to believe that people don't like you because your mother came from Mexico. The only real reason people don't like you is yourself, Juanita. Your job isn't to change your grandmother—it's to change *you*. So don't try to blame anyone else."

And with that Mom stood up, brushed the crumbs from her Levi's, and looked at the mountains around her.

"It's going to storm," she said. "It's going to storm hard."

Angie discovered that she had been holding her breath. She let it out in a rush and looked around their little mountain hollow. Because of her absorption in what was happening before her, she had forgotten the spectacular mountain drama that could rise so quickly in Colorado. What had been the usual dark cloud over otherwise sunny mountains had suddenly boiled over to hide the snow saddle peaks. She could hear the wind and the rain roaring and pounding down the slopes from a distance. The grass fluttered as if a hand stroked it, and then bent almost flat before the force of the wind. Even as she watched, the first raindrops stung her face.

Frantically the three scooped up their picnic things and ran for the nearest clump of pine trees. Breathlessly they crouched behind the trunks, pulling up jackets to shield their heads and shoulders. Mom clasped an arm about each girl and pulled them close to her and they huddled together for warmth against the icy pellets of rain. Angie put out her hand and the pellets stung with a force that hurt and bounced into the air.

"Hail," Jinx said.

Lightning speared the sky and its prongs struck a nearby slope with a deafening thunderclap which crashed and echoed among the peaks. There was an awful majesty about black clouds and jagged peaks as they seemed to war with each other.

"We can't stay here under these exposed trees," Jinx said. "We'll be safer where there's a whole forest. We've got to run for it."

They stumbled into the open and scurried for the pine forest while hail lashed them with stinging needles. Then hail turned to rain and never in all her life had Angie seen such rain. There were no separate drops. It was as if a gigantic pail had been tipped over in the skies, flooding the mountainsides with sheets of water. Above the heads of the three the pines moaned and twanged in the storm. Jackets were as soaked as the rest of them in a moment's time. Under their feet the rusty pine needles turned sodden as a swamp. And all about lightning played among the mountains and ferocious claps of thunder roused the echoes.

Angie whimpered and drew closer to her mother. It was the noise that terrified her more than anything else, while the cold and discomfort undermined her normal courage. Jinx clung to no one. She stood within the circle of Mom's protecting arm, but she did not lean against her. She merely watched, white-faced, while the rain came down in endless sheets.

Despite her own misery, Angie couldn't help wondering what Jinx was thinking about, couldn't help feeling a little sorry for her because of the word lashing Mom had given her. If anyone ever talked to her like that, Angie thought, she'd just want to crawl away and die. But maybe Jinx was made of sterner stuff, and maybe Mom knew it. She saw that her mother glanced at the other girl anxiously now and then, but made no attempt to speak to her.

That Jinx was thinking long thoughts of her own became evident when she turned suddenly and spoke to Angie.

"I read that newspaper," she said.

Angie gave her a watery look of bewilderment, the rain slippery wet on her face. "What newspaper?"

"The one in that breadbox you dug up. Before I burned it. There was a piece in it marked in blue pencil."

Angie couldn't have been less interested at the moment, but she listened because Jinx seemed to be ridding herself of some sense of guilt by telling her.

"It was a piece about the time when my father was killed by a rock fall in the Blossom mine. It said he'd been looking in the mine because he believed there was pitchblende there. But after his death, Grandpa closed everything up and wouldn't let anybody look."

Mom paid no attention to this talk. Her red hair was plastered tight against her head and rain dripped off her nose and ran down her chin. Once she shook her head like a wet dog and then looked anxiously at Jinx.

"Do you think we ought to stay here, Juanita? The thunder has moved off, though it's raining just as hard as ever. We can't get any wetter. Don't you think we'd better go home?"

Jinx started off like a small dog that had been held at the leash. "Come along," she called. "Let's hurry!"

Angie couldn't see much sense to the pace Jinx set them. They were soaked and cold and miserable and not even fast walking was going to warm them up. So why try for a breathless pace that had them stumbling, gasping for breath?

"Wait, Juanita!" Mom called at last. "Angie and I can't keep up with you. There's no need for such a rush. We're not racing for shelter, goodness knows!"

Jinx was a couple of yards ahead of them and she whirled around at Mom's words and Angie saw that her eyes were wide with fright in her white face.

"It's raining too hard too long!" she cried. "Can't you find your way if I go ahead and leave you here? The trail's clear."

But Mom meant to take no chances of getting lost in these mountains without a guide.

"We must stay together," she said firmly. "Let's stop for a moment and get our breath. Then we'll go on. But I can't see why the rush is necessary."

Jinx came back to them. "We can't tell what's happening down in the canyon. I want to get where I can see."

"What's the good of that?" Mom asked. "There isn't anything we can do."

Jinx turned on her impatiently. "Grandpa's told me what can happen. A gulch or a canyon can act like a chimney. Warm air rushes up in a draft and it holds the cold air up there for a while until it gets too heavy with water. Then the whole thing breaks and rain goes crashing down every gulch and canyon and watershed. That's what makes a flash flood."

"Blossom?" Mom demanded tensely. "Do you mean Blossom might be in danger?"

"I don't know," Jinx said. "Oh, do let's go on!"

They hurried as fast as they could go after that. Angie's heart pounded in her chest and her breath wheezed in her lungs, but fear drove her on. The mud of the trail clung to her shoes, making them heavy, and water squished inside them at every step. Finally the trail began to emerge from the dripping, dark green world of pines and the way lightened ahead. Miraculously, there was sunlight and green mountains and the usual puffs of white cloud against a sapphire sky.

They stepped out into the warm, dry world with a sense of unreality. It seemed hard to believe that here the storm had not so much as dampened a blade of grass. In her relief that it was over, Angie turned her best cartwheel and lighted squishing wet, but right side up, to smile at the white-faced Jinx.

Jinx did not return her smile. "It's still raining back there. Do come along! We've got to hurry!"

But Angie couldn't feel as frightened with the sun drying her clothes and shining brightly on a world where no lightning licked the mountains and no thunder crashed about their ears. Mom hurried on after Jinx and Angie followed them, moving less breathlessly now.

The path dipped steeply and in a few moments they saw ahead of them the pinnacles of red rock that jutted out at the place far above the meeting of gulch and creek canyon. Angie ran ahead to join Jinx as she climbed up the rocky crag and this time Mom did not call her back, but came too, climbing after them.

The rough rock offered ledges for their feet, and notches for fingers to grasp, and there was a castellated top where they could stand and look down over the red ramparts. Jinx was there first, Angie next, and a moment later Mom stood beside them.

The view was tremendous, breath-taking, with the deep gash of the canyon far below, and above, the ranges marching away into blue distance. But Angie wasted no more than a single glance at the grandeur about her. She followed the direction of Jinx's pointing finger.

Down in the canyon Blossom Creek was a strong yellow stream, lapping the banks near the road, splashing the sides of the canyon. But it was not, apparently, in the condition Jinx feared to see because she sighed and sat limply down on a ledge of rock.

"Maybe everything will be all right," she said. "If only it stops raining back there soon enough."

Angie moved to a point where she could glimpse the black mountains where the storm still rumbled. A distant roaring that was not thunder, but was like nothing she had ever heard, came to her ears. Jinx heard it too and was at her side in a moment, peering toward the place where a bend in the canyon hid the upper creek from view.

They saw it clearly as it crashed around the bend—a high, muddy wall of water, tossing great trees on its crest as if they had been twigs, tumbling giant boulders down from the canyon side. The roof of a house bobbed for an instant above the surface front and then boiled under as the wall crashed on down the canyon.

Angie screamed in terror, and Mom's arm came hard and tight about her. But they could only stand there helplessly, far above the wall of destruction that was moving relentlessly down upon Blossom.

17

The Blue Box

Mom was the first to move. She scrambled down the
outcropping of rock, slipping part of the way,
scratching a long red welt along one arm. Jinx and Angie were after her in a moment.

"We've got to get to Blossom!" Mom cried, her voice
cracking on a thin, high note that didn't sound like her
at all.

Jinx stumbled after her as if she could hardly see the
way. "There isn't any Blossom. But we have to get
there anyway."

The roar of wild, tumbling waters far below was already lessening as the crest of the wall pounded down
Blossom Creek.

As she followed the other two, Angie began to cry in
deep, shaking sobs that caught her breath. No tears
came—just sobbing breaths. Jinx heard her and turned
back, her own eyes dry, though her voice trembled.

"You stop that, Angela!" she said surprisingly.
"We've got to get down there and see if there's anything we can do. And whatever's happened, your mom
needs you plenty now."

She didn't wait for Angie's reaction, but ran on to
help Mom, who had stumbled over a root and fallen to
her knees. Ashamed, Angie hurried to help too and
Mom clung to them both while she pulled herself to her
feet. A great tear had ripped the knee of her Levi's and
she had rubbed blood on her face from a jagged cut on
her hand. But she seemed unaware of her hurts, hardly

aware of the two girls. Her whole being was bound up in an urgent effort to get down that mountain trail with the utmost speed.

It was Jinx who halted her headlong flight. She caught Mom by the arm to pull her back, and Jinx was strong and muscular.

"Maybe they'll need us," Jinx said earnestly. "We won't be much good if we kill ourselves on the way down."

A look of reason came into Mom's eyes, and though she turned back to the trail at once, she moved at a less reckless pace and let Jinx go ahead. Angie followed on their heels, troubled memories flashing through her mind as she put one sodden foot after the other in the flight downhill.

Memories of young Jasper and Gold Strike fighting over Mr. Gimmore. Of Mark, holding up a black stone for her to see. And then, with a pain that knotted somewhere inside her, came the memory of her father's hand, holding her own so tight and firm that night when Grandpa Kobler played his guitar and sang mountain melodies. She'd felt so safe then with her hand in his strong clasp.

Now and then the path broke toward the mountain's edge and they could see down into the canyon where yellow water poured in a high, seething flood. The road was gone from view. Any car traveling it would have been swept into the stream. There were soft places where the force of the water had undermined the hill and tons of earth had slid down into the creek bed, leaving a raw scar on the hillside behind.

It seemed hours before they reached a place from which they could see Blossom itself—or what had once been the town of Blossom. The narrow valley had turned into a roaring river in which debris tumbled and tossed. Timbers and rooftops and broken bits of houses boiled up and under and up again. No living thing could have fought that current and come out alive. Yet still they must stumble on, in the thin hope that somehow those they loved had escaped disaster.

Angie saw her mother's lips move silently as she stared at the flood below and knew that she was praying. Angie prayed too—though it was a frantic prayer, without coherent words or sense. When Mom started down the path again, Jinx stopped her.

"We can't get down that way. The trail has been washed out. Let's follow the hillside to where we can get a better view—over near the mine." Angie flung a backward look toward distant mountains before she followed the others. The sky was serenely blue. All storm clouds had vanished and the rain had stopped. But too late, far too late, to save poor little Blossom.

On they went along the hillside, following its irregularities, climbing over rocks, winding through pines and aspen, then out into the open again, until once more Jinx halted.

"Look," she said.

Angie stared and saw that part of the hill ahead had been undermined so that a great landslide had spilled down the mountainside.

"The mine," Jinx said, "the mine is gone!"

Angie understood then. Gone was the shaft house and the opening into the mine. Everything had been buried under tons of rock and earth. But Angie could feel no emotion looking at the changed face of the mountain. The mine was of no concern to her now.

"Listen!" Mom cried, an electric note in her voice.

Jinx and Angie held their breath. The river that flowed through Blossom did not roar so loudly now. The waters were spending themselves, rushing out through the gap at the far end of the valley. But above their rush and hiss came another sound—the unmistakable sound of human voices.

It was Angie this time who broke into a run on the mountainside. Ahead, climbing over a hump of rock, came a small procession: first Dad, with young Jasper on one arm and a sheaf of yellow manuscript pages— his book!—in his free hand. Behind him came Mark, carrying Dad's portable typewriter in one hand and in the other the blue metal box that belonged to Bill

Rolfe. Just the three of them. No one else. But in that moment no one else mattered to Angie and her mother.

Dad dropped Jasper unceremoniously to the ground and caught Angie in his arms for a great quick hug, before he put her aside and held Mom close to him, where she could hide her face against his shoulder and cling to him weeping. Angie picked up Jasper, who looked bewildered by all this crying and hugging, and squeezed him so hard that he yelped. At the same time she smiled at Mark with misty eyes.

It was Dad who looked over Mom's red head at Jinx, who stood watching this reunion with dark grave eyes. Dad took one arm from about Mom and held out a hand.

"Come here, Juanita," he said, while Mom caught Jasper away from Angie and kissed him thoroughly, much to his all-boy indignation.

Jinx stayed where she was, staring at Dad with a forlorn look that it broke Angie's heart to see.

"Grandpa?" Jinx said. "And my grandmother?"

"I wish I could tell you," Dad said gently. "But we don't know. When the warning came, your grandfather was already on his way to the cemetery on the other side of the valley. So your grandmother went after him. The cemetery is on higher ground. If they reached it, they are probably safe."

"Was there time to reach it?" Jinx asked.

"I don't know," Dad said. "I—I'm afraid not."

Jinx turned away and went to sit on a rock where she could look down at the waters that flowed through Blossom. Angie would have gone after her, but Mom caught her back.

"No, honey," she whispered. "Let her be for now. This is something she has to face alone."

So they let Jinx be, while Dad and Mark poured out a somewhat scrambled story of what had happened. Some ranchers up above the canyon had seen the danger, seen the waters piling up, spilling down the gulches and watersheds to swell the force of water in the canyon. One of them had come racing down by car, no more than ten minutes ahead of the wall of water, to warn the valley dwellers of their danger.

"I was out in the yard, playing with Jasper, and Bill Rolfe was there too," Mark said. "The rancher wanted Bill to come along and help warn folks that live down the next valley. So Bill handed me his box to look after, and took our station wagon and followed the rancher's car. Gosh, I hope they made it all right!"

"And then Mark called me," Dad took up the story. "So I picked up my manuscript and Jasper, while Mark tore down the road to tell Grandmother Kobler, and then the three of us climbed up past the mine and got to a high place where we would be safe. It's a good thing we didn't stay near the mine—the whole mountain caved in and slid down. It will take some digging to uncover that mine again."

"The waters are beginning to go down," Jinx said, standing up on her rock.

The Wetherals joined her and looked down into the valley. Sure enough, as the force behind it lessened, and the bulk of the flood rushed out of the gap at the bottom of the valley, the muddy level was lowered, sucking down along the banks, leaving mud and debris and wreckage behind it.

In one place a rounded tower rose above the water. That was the cupola on the Kobler house, so that house, at least, had not been tumbled off its foundations and whirled away. But as time passed and the waters went down, the heartbreaking truth was revealed. Hardly a board was left standing in Blossom. The landslide from the mine had buried the school so that not a stone of it could be seen. Of the house Uncle Ben had left the Wetherals, not a stray board remained. The tipsy little bandstand was gone completely. Only old Shadrach, standing strong and proud in the dignity of years, had withstood the force of the flood. But his handsome blue branches were filled with wreckage, and mud plastered him three quarters of the way to his high top.

"The jail's still there," Mark said, "but all the business buildings are gone. Blossom's really a ghost town now and we're refugees." He seemed to like that idea, so he repeated it. "That's what we are—refugees. We haven't anything left at all."

"We have us," Mom told him. "And that's all that really matters."

"Besides," said Angie sensibly, "we still have all our things down in Boulder. We've only lost our camping stuff and some old clothes. We have a place to go, and probably Bill Rolfe or someone will come back to get us."

"Mr. Gimmore gone!" announced Jasper suddenly, and Angie remembered that long, long ago—this morning—the giraffe hadn't been found and no one had troubled to look for him. So now Mr. Waldo Gimmore was a flood victim too. For the first time Angie remembered the little skunk. Poor Gold Strike, who liked to sleep in the daytime, would never have had a chance in that water.

They sat on the rocky ground and watched the river that had once been Blossom Creek. After Jinx had asked two or three times if they couldn't do *something,* and Dad had said there was nothing to do, Mark got up and wandered restlessly off a little way up the hill. A few minutes later he shouted down to Angie.

"Come up here! Come up here quick!"

Even Jinx was caught by his insistent tone and when Angie started up the hill after her brother, Jinx came too. When they reached Mark, he pointed across the steep slide of earth that hid what had once been the mine.

"Look over there," he commanded. "Look over there and see if you see what I think I see."

Angie and Jinx stared. Angie's eyes searched among the boulders and humps of the slope that lay beyond the landslide, but Jinx saw what he meant first. "By the cave!" she cried. "Right in front of the cave!"

Angie found the place and gasped. There in the dry, safe, entrance to the cave, far above the water, and untouched by the slide, stood a small black-and-white creature with a wavy tail that spilled over his back in plumes. It was Gold Strike. And in his mouth he held a dilapidated something or other that could only be—yes it was!

"It's Mr. Gimmore!" Angie cried, and for some reason felt ridiculously happy to know that both the little skunk and the toy giraffe had not been lost in the flood. Probably Gold Strike had gone up there that morning for his sleep and had taken the giraffe along.

Already Jinx was climbing up the hill and Mark started after her.

"We can climb around the top of the landslide and get over there," he said.

Angie pointed to the box Mark still carried. "Don't take Bill's box along. Leave it here."

But Mark shook his head. "He trusted me with it. He said not to let it out of my hands, and I'm not going to."

"Well, then," Angie suggested, "let's have a look at what's inside. I've always wanted to know."

Mark thought about that solemnly for a moment as they climbed the hill. "I guess it would be all right. He never told me not to open it. He just said to take care of it. I tell you what—when we get over to the cave, we'll open it."

As they skirted the top of the slide, Angie found that now that she knew her family were safe, her interest in the mine had returned. And with interest came a sense of loss. Buried beneath all these tons of earth lay Uncle Ben's treasure. The clipping Jinx had burned was the last determining clue. But now they could never reach the mine to prove the existence of pitchblende in its tunnels, and no grownup would ever believe in their story enough to go to the expense of digging through the rubble. It didn't matter so much any more for the Wetherals themselves. As Dad had pointed out, the mine wouldn't belong to them anyway. But it mattered terribly because of Jinx. This mountainside might belong to the Koblers. And if Grandpa and Grandmother Kobler had been—but her mind turned sickly away from that thought. Jinx was scrambling eagerly toward the cave in Mark's wake, and Angie hurried after them.

Gold Strike put Mr. Gimmore behind him and watched their approach suspiciously. As they came nearer, he growled low in his throat and stamped his front feet in a warning that he would protect his property. But as that did not stop them, he whirled around, picked up the giraffe in his mouth, and carried it into the cave. A moment later he poked his black little nose out and regarded them with interest. Now that Mr. Gimmore was safely hidden, he seemed glad enough to see them, and when Jinx held out her hands and called to him, he bounced over to her joyfully. Jinx caught the little animal to her and hugged him as if he were all she had left in the world. Mark, however, was more interested in Bill Rolfe's blue box. He sat down in front of the cave and put the box on the ground before him.

"What do you suppose is in it?" he said, dragging things out dramatically as usual.

"Well, go ahead and open it!" Angie urged. "There are only two little catches and it will take two seconds to open them."

Mark relented and clicked open the catches. Then he raised the lid to reveal a set of dials and knobs and a pair of earphones. Whatever Angie had expected, it wasn't this.

"It's only a portable radio," she said in disappointment. "Now why do you suppose he carried that around with him? I never heard him play it."

Mark shook his head and fiddled with the dials. "It's not a radio. At least I don't think it is."

He unwound the cords of the earphones and put them on. Then, while Angie watched, he turned a switch, a thoughtful expression on his face.

"Well?" Angie asked. "Do you hear anything?"

"Sure," he said. "Want to listen?" He took off the phones and handed them to her.

She fitted them over her ears and listened intently. But all she heard was a clicking sound, with the clicks spaced far apart.

"It's not tuned in," she protested. "I'm not getting anything."

"What do you expect—bop?" Mark asked. "I told you it wasn't a radio. But I think I know what it is. Let me have the phones again."

Jinx set Gold Strike down and he promptly set to work to lick his shiny black fur to a still higher state of gloss. She paid no attention to Mark and the blue box, but stood up so that she could look down once more on the mud plain that had once been Blossom.

Angie gave the earphones back to Mark and watched while he listened again to the faint clicking sound.

"What's it for, Mark?" she pleaded. "Tell me!"

But he didn't tell her. He moved the box around in different directions, held it to a nearby rock, carried it into the cave. Then he looked out at her, his eyes dancing with excitement.

"Come here," he called. "Come here and listen."

She crawled into the little cave beside him and put on the earphones again. This time the clicking was so loud and fast it sounded like radio static in a thunderstorm. She stared at her brother, puzzled.

"It *is* a radio and I'm not getting anything but static."

"Girls are so dumb," Mark said, taking the phones away from her and putting them on. "Golly, just listen to that! It's got to mean something. Angie, don't you know what this is? It's a Geiger counter! I've read about them, though I never saw one before. There's always what they call a background count of clicks that don't mean anything. But when they come as fast and close together as this—there's only one answer."

Angie waited breathlessly.

"Radioactive ores," Mark said. "Pitchblende ... uranium!"

After listening again and moving the blue box around in the cave, Mark took off the phones.

"Let's look back inside the cave," he said.

Angie had never paid much attention to the inside

before, except to note that there always seemed to be a faint draft that came out from behind the broken-up rock wall at the back. Now Mark got down on his hands and knees and crawled close to the rear wall. He poked around a little and a few broken chunks of rock came loose and clattered to the floor of the cave. Mark reached in his hand and pulled out something limp and dangly. It was Mr. Gimmore. Gold Strike had evidently figured out a new hiding place.

Angie, however, had picked up one of the broken bits of rock that had tumbled out at her feet. It was heavy and looked and felt just like the chunks Uncle Ben had hidden in the breadbox. While Mark put on the phones, she held the stone close to the blue box. By Mark's expression she knew the impulses must be coming thick and fast.

Angie laughed softly. "Jasper was certainly right— Mr. Gimmore *knew*." She crawled to the entrance of the cave and looked out at Jinx. "Do you suppose this cave could lead back into one of the tunnels of the mine?" she asked. "Maybe that's why a draft seems to come out of the mountain."

Jinx might as well have been deaf for all the attention she paid to Angie's question. "I'm going down," she said. "There's a place where the bridge used to be where I think I can get across. I'm going over to the cemetery."

18

Letter from Uncle Ben

Angie called Mark quickly. They couldn't let Jinx go down alone. But by the time her brother had crawled out of the cave, Jinx was already scrambling down the hill, choosing a route that circled the buried schoolhouse. Angie cupped her hands about her mouth and shouted across to Dad, indicating what Jinx was about to attempt. He called, but when Jinx paid no attention, he too started down the hill.

They all met at the edge of the mud flat below. Jinx was already taking off her shoes and socks and the others followed her example. Dad rolled up his trousers, warned Angie and Mark to be careful, and set off through the squishy mud after Jinx. The whole valley had a strange, dank, mucky smell now, instead of the spicy odor of pines.

The place where the bridge had been was on higher ground than the rest and, while the bridge itself had been swept away, there were enough old boards and timber that could be salvaged to throw across the gap to make a footbridge. It was a rickety bridge, with no sides, and close beneath it Blossom Creek poured foaming, muddy water. Angie fixed her gaze on the far bank and crossed quickly, holding onto Dad's jacket, trying not to look down at the waters that almost lapped her bare feet. From the hill behind she could hear her mother calling something, but the wind carried away the words. Anyway, they couldn't go back now. They had to go on and try to help Jinx.

The moment she reached the other bank, Jinx began to shout, "Grandpa! Grandpa!" but no answer reached them except the wailing of the pines.

Cool, wet mud oozed between Angie's toes, but she discovered quickly that it couldn't be trusted. Anywhere she stepped there might be hidden stones or broken boards. At least bare feet made travel possible, where shoes would only have burdened them by collecting mud.

The road dipped up and down in its winding approach to the cemetery. Angie was walking at Jinx's side when the road turned and dipped toward a hollow still filled with high water. She saw what Jinx saw in the very same instant. For a moment the two girls stood where they were, too surprised to move.

Down in the hollow, neck deep in water, stood Grandmother Kobler. At first glance Angie thought she was alone. Then she saw that the old woman was supporting the weight of another person in her arms. Her face was gray and strained, and you knew that she stood there grimly with her very last strength. She was too weak to call out to them, but somehow she had managed to hold Grandpa Kobler's head above the water. Apparently the protecting hills about the hollow had saved them from the full rush and tumble of the flood.

Dad and Mark and Jinx plunged straight into the yellow water and waded and swam out to the two in the center. Angie stood on the bank, where Dad told her to stay, and danced around in anxiety and excitement. Grandpa Kobler was unconscious, but Dad and Mark between them managed to bring him out of the water and up to higher ground, where they could lay him on ground that was dry and untouched by the flood.

Jinx put an arm around her grandmother, supporting her with one strong little shoulder, and coaxed the old lady with gentle words until she turned dazedly toward the shore. Angie held out her hands to help, and between them they half dragged, half propelled Grandmother Kobler toward drier ground. She could not make it to Grandpa Kobler's side, however, but sank to her knees before she reached him.

Before Jinx could rush off to her grandfather, Mrs. Kobler reached weakly out to touch her hand. "I knew you'd come, Juanita," she said. "I've been thinking and thinking, standing out there in the water. And I knew you'd come."

Jinx looked at her for a moment. Then with a sudden quick gesture she flung her arms about her grandmother's neck. "You held Grandpa up! You held him up all that time!"

For a moment the two clung together, each needing the other for the first time. Then Grandmother Kobler gave Jinx a little push. "Go see how he is. I'm afraid for him. Terribly afraid."

Jinx hurried to the other group and Grandmother Kobler lay back against the sloping hill and closed her eyes. Somewhere off in the distance there were calls and shouts. Dad, who had been kneeling beside Grandpa Kobler, stood up and shouted back.

"That's Bill Rolfe!" Mark cried. "He's brought help!" And he and Angie and Jinx added their own clamor to guide Bill up to them.

A couple of ranchers had come with him and they had brought medical supplies in case of need. One of them administered stimulants to both the old people and the gray color left Grandmother Kobler's face. In no time at all, as her strength returned, she began to direct the matter of improvising a stretcher of sticks and jackets on which Grandpa could be carried. Angie watched in amazed admiration. Jinx and her grandmother had something of the same quality of courage and capability when great need arose. The old man opened his eyes and seemed to know them, but his breathing was faint and it was necessary to get him to a warm bed as quickly as possible.

The hike into the next valley was hard going. Dad climbed the hill again on the other side of the creek and brought Jasper and Mom down. Even Gold Strike

joined the procession and Angie picked him up and
carried him. The domesticated little animal belonged
with his human friends. Grandmother Kobler remembered the old cow on the high meadow and one of the
ranchers promised to take care of her.

They all walked in single file, plowing through the
sticky mud, sometimes finding a place where they could
move more swiftly on dry ground along the hill.

Angie couldn't see how Grandmother Kobler managed it, but some second surge of strength seemed to
flow through the old woman, and she followed close behind Grandpa's stretcher, leaning on Jinx with one
hand, but never falling behind.

There was a moment, just before the stumbling little
file went down through the gap into the next valley,
when Jinx paused and looked back toward the place
that had once been the town of Blossom. Only the jail
and the battered Kobler house remained standing. All
the rest was ugly ruin.

"We'll come back," Jinx whispered fiercely. "Somehow we'll come back!"

Angie saw Grandmother Kobler's hand tighten on
Jinx's shoulder. "No, we won't, Juanita. We won't, because God has other plans. Better plans than we could
make."

Jinx threw her grandmother a look of surprise, and
then hurried on to catch up with the stretcher.

Not until they reached the next valley and a house
high enough on the hill to be untouched by the flood
did the old woman give in and allow herself to be put
to bed.

By the next day Grandpa Kobler was seriously ill
and exhaustion had caught up with Mrs. Kobler. The
ranch people got an ambulance up from Boulder and
the two old ones were able to travel comfortably down
to the Boulder hospital.

So, after all, Jinx came to stay for a while with the
Wetherals. Dad went eagerly back to work on his book.
He had his big climax scene now in which a flash flood
poured down the mountains on his ghost town and

Guthridge Gilmore, at the risk of his own life, captured the murderer singlehanded.

Mark and Angie and Bill Rolfe had more realistic business. With Bill's help they convinced Mr. Bingham that a discovery of real importance had been made on the hillside above Blossom, and in due time, when Grandpa Kobler was convalescing and had been warned that he must not return to mountain life, they all met one night in the big living room of the house on Baseline Road. The Wetherals were there, including Jasper and Mr. Gimmore—now minus both ears; and the Koblers, Gold Strike, and even Bill Rolfe.

Mr. Bingham said that the conditions of an important discovery had been fully met. Samples of ore had been sent to the Bureau of Mines in Salt Lake City, and a man from the A.E.C.—the Atomic Energy Commission—had come out to Blossom. This vein of pitchblende was an important find of real value to the country. So Mr. Bingham had opened Uncle Ben's sealed envelope, and they were all meeting here today while he divulged its contents.

The story was much as they had imagined. Uncle Ben had discovered the vein of pitchblende in a forgotten tunnel of the old mine. Jinx's father had suspected its existence years later, but had directed his search toward the wrong section of the mine and had met his death. In the beginning Uncle Ben had thought only in terms of radium. Later, after the war, when the full value of uranium was known, he became aware of the true worth of his "treasure." But his own life had made him something of an eccentric and he had curious notions about the revealing of this particular treasure. From his letter they gathered that he alternated between not wanting it to be found because of what riches did to some men, and feeling that someone who worked for it might be entitled to profit from it. So he walled up the tunnel with chunks of rock, and amused himself by burying the breadbox with its clues and making his little "maps" to pass out to his friends.

But, now that the secret was known, he wanted to

will the entire mine to Juanita Kobler, in the keeping of her grandparents until she was of age.

They were all sitting around the living room, listening intently. Grandpa Kobler was propped up against pillows on the couch, Grandmother in a chair nearby with sewing in her lap as usual, and Jinx on the floor at her grandfather's feet. Bill Rolfe played with Jasper and Gold Strike, and Mr. Gimmore, more faded than ever, and thin from loss of stuffing, smiled at them happily from under a table.

Angie was thrilled for Jinx's sake—Juanita, as Mom said they must learn to call her. The mountain girl had been blossoming under Mom's love and attention. She was discovering that she was someone in her own right and forgetting her foolish notions. Her grandmother seemed to be giving her a new respect. More than once Grandmother Kobler had spoken of the long thoughts that had come to her during those hours after she and Grandpa Kobler had been caught by the rising waters of the flood—hours when she had stood there talking to God, asking for his help. She hadn't changed her prejudices—Mom said she probably wouldn't because she was too old. But she was remembering now the thing she had so long forgotten—that Juanita was her son's daughter too.

But in spite of all these things that were so fine for Juanita, Angie couldn't help a feeling of disappointment. Somehow it seemed a little unfair that when it had been their own persistence that had uncovered the secret, there was nothing to be had from all this for the Wetherals—for Dad.

Mr. Bingham cleared his throat and looked directly at Angie, and she saw that his mouth had cracked into a funny sort of smile.

"I owe you an apology, young lady," he said. "If I had listened to you that day, all this might have been under way before now. Of course you and your brother will get more than apology. The reward, of course, is yours."

"Reward?" cried Angie and Mark together.

"Sure," Bill Rolfe put in. "What do you suppose I was up there in the hills prospecting for if it wasn't that ten thousand dollars the Government gives for finding ores that assay twenty per cent or more uranium oxide? Pitchblende is from sixty to ninety per cent pure uranium."

Angie and Mark looked at each other. Angie said, "Ten thousand dollars!" in a voice that came out a squawk. "Why—with ten thousand dollars we can—"

"It's not all ours," Mark said quickly. "There's that blue box, you know."

Angie knew he was right. If it hadn't been for Bill's Geiger counter, the treasure would be just as far away as ever, and she was as quick as Mark to offer Bill his share. But in the end Bill wouldn't take a fifty-fifty split, and it was decided that the reward, when it was paid, would be divided three ways, with two thirds going to the Wetherals, since Angie and Mark had done most of the work, and one third for Bill Rolfe.

That night after dinner, when Mr. Bingham had gone, and Angie and Juanita had finished wiping Mom's dishes, the two girls wandered into the living room to find Dad standing by the picture window. All the lamps were off and he was watching the lights of Boulder with the line of foothills rising above them.

The other Wetherals knew what it meant when Dad stood by a window in the dark, looking out and thinking.

Mom put her head in from the kitchen and said, "Oh-oh, I'll bet Guthridge Gilmore has spotted another crime!"

Dad shook his head. "Guthridge Gilmore has retired on a pension. If the rest of my family are willing, we'll look for a house of our own in Boulder and settle down to some serious writing."

Mark gave one of his wild whoops, but Angie hardly heard him because Juanita's hand had reached out half shyly to touch her arm.

"Then we'll both be staying here," Juanita said. "Grandpa wants a little house here in Boulder where he

can be close to the mountains. We'll be going to the
same school. So I—I'll have a friend."

"And I'll have a friend," Angie said quickly. "We'll
both be new, but we'll be starting together. Just
think—for my very best friend I'll have the heiress to
the Blossom fortune, the beautiful daughter of the romantic—"

Juanita laughed out loud. "Oh, you hush!" she cried,
sounding not at all like the little mountain "critter" of
Blossom.

Young Jasper had been ignored long enough. He
crawled out from under a table, yanking the giraffe by
his wobbly neck.

"Mr. Gimmore knows!" he announced, using his old
bid for attention.

But no one listened to him because now they all
knew—knew about the black diamonds that were no
longer the hidden treasure of Blossom, Colorado.

Other SIGNET Books You'll Enjoy